Zarkon, Lord of the Unknown
THE NEMESIS OF EVIL

BOOKS BY LIN CARTER

THE MAN WHO LOVED MARS
THE CITY OUTSIDE THE WORLD
LOST WORLDS
KESRICK

Zarkon, Lord of the Unknown

THE NEMESIS OF EVIL
INVISIBLE DEATH
THE VOLCANO OGRE
THE EARTH SHAKER

The Chronicles of Kylix

THE QUEST OF KADJI
THE WIZARD OF ZAO

The Adventures of Thongor

THONGOR AND THE WIZARD OF LEMURIA
THONGOR AND THE DRAGON CITY
THONGOR AGAINST THE GODS
THONGOR IN THE CITY OF MAGICIANS
THONGOR AT THE END OF TIME

The Adventures of Eric Carstairs in Zanthodon

JOURNEY TO THE UNDERGROUND WORLD
HUROK OF THE STONE AGE
DARYA OF THE BRONZE AGE
ERIC OF ZANTHODON

The Gondwane Epic

THE WARRIOR OF WORLD'S END
THE ENCHANTRESS OF WORLD'S END
THE IMMORTAL OF WORLD'S END
THE BARBARIAN OF WORLD'S END
THE PIRATE OF WORLD'S END

Terra Magica

MANDRICARDO
CALLIPYGIA
DRAGONROUGE

Zarkon, Lord of the Unknown
THE NEMESIS OF EVIL

LIN CARTER

WILDSIDE PRESS
BERKELEY HEIGHTS, NJ • 1999

THE NEMESIS OF EVIL

Published by:

Wildside Press
P.O. Box 45
Gillette, NJ 07933-0045
www.wildsidepress.com

ISBN: 1-58715-057-3

NOTE:

After three years of trying off and on through an old high school friend now in the U. S. House of Representatives, and a college buddy now serving in the Department of Justice, I have finally succeeded in obtaining the permission of the Omega organization to write up in book form several of the most outstanding cases in which that little-known crime-fighting group crossed blades with super-criminals.

This book and those that will follow have, frankly, been heavily fictionalized. That is, I have invented dialog and the descriptions, from the expressions on the faces of the characters to their hair color. But, to a surprising degree, everything else in this book and its sequels is exact, literal truth.

It is fact, not fiction, despite the official "category" into which my publishers will place these books in their catalogs.

I have re-created the events that follow through the medium of exhaustive tape-recorded interviews with the Omega men themselves. By cross-referral of the memories of the men who participated in these events, I have arrived at what seems to me a vivid, detailed, highly accurate synthesis of the actual event. But I have not scrupled to invent where memory fails and where invention serves the crispness and immediate impact of each scene, remembering the novelist's tenet: *Make it seem real.*

One thing more. Without exception, every single name in this book is fictitious. Not only the names of every character, but also the names of places and institutions. There is no newspaper called the *Illustrated Press* in Los Angeles. If there has ever existed, or exists now, anywhere in the world, a cult or mystical order named "the Brotherhood of Lemurian Wisdom," I am innocent of any knowledge of the fact, and tender them my apologies in advance.

There is no country in Europe called Novenia, no suburb of Palma Laguna known as Seagrove, and, as I'm sure my reader knows, no city or town on the Eastern Seaboard called Knickerbocker City. Prince Zarkon's true name is not "Prince Zarkon," and the *real* Omega organization is not known as "the Omega organization."

The reason behind my substitution of invented names for those of the actual individuals and institutions involved in the story is quite a simple one. The amazing man whom I have chosen to call "Prince Zarkon" insisted on the practice, as a condition of granting the series of lengthy interviews I requested. His reasons for asking this seem obvious to me: to protect the names and reputations of all persons involved in the story and to ensure the continuing operations of himself and his lieutenants. The less that is known about them and their organization, the less vulnerable they are to their enemies. (And, incidentally, let me say, here and now, that the account of Prince Zarkon's secret origin as given in Chapter 23 is *completely fictitious*; I felt something of the sort was required in order to motivate this character, to explain logically his reason for adopting so extraordinary a career. His real reason is not known to me.)

I have gone to these lengths, all this trouble, because I am a trifle bored with writing sensational fiction. Impressed by true crime documentaries such as Truman Capote's *In Cold Blood*, I felt inspired to try my hand at the "non-fiction novel," an exciting new story form which Capote more or less invented. The result is in your hands, and if, perchance, it reads more like a *novel*-novel than a *non-fiction* novel, the credit rests with the sequence of events rather than with my skill or artistry in reporting them.

Readers who know my own fiction, and thus know me fairly well, will understand why I felt drawn to this kind of a narrative rather than to the sort of story which appealed to Mr. Capote. I like to write crisp, vivid, exciting stories filled with color and action, and I like to read that sort of thing, too. Hence I felt instinctively attracted to the cases of Omega, because that's the sort of adventures they have.

This is, by the way, the case reported in File 12 of Omega, the twelfth case upon which Zarkon and his organization embarked. The events took place in early August 1970. You will search the newspapers of that month in vain for anything remotely resembling the narrative I have written here: For reasons that will become obvious as you read the story, most of it was officially unreported. But those who seek will find. And the unexplained death of an unidentified man wearing red robes found at the base of Mount Shasta, the surprise arrest of several criminals on the FBI's "most wanted" list, and a few other events on the periphery of this story can actually be found in the public press of the time, however inadequately explained. Look 'em up for yourself, if you don't believe me.

I do not myself know the actual name or real

identity of the brilliant but deranged scientific criminal called "Lucifer" in these pages. But that name, as well as "Zandor Sinestro," are my inventions.

Since the Omega organization goes, and has ever gone, to extraordinary lengths to conceal the very fact of its existence, and has continually discouraged publicity rather than seeking it, some account of how I first heard of Omega and first got on its trail seems called for. I am no sleuth, no investigative reporter, like the ill-fated MacAndrews of File 12, but by an odd quirk of fate I became involved in one of Omega's cases a few years ago while returning from an overlong visit to Cambodia with my wife.

My role in that adventure was certainly a minor one (I am no man of action, only a writer), so I will say nothing about it here; besides, the Justice Department has asked me not to discuss that particular sequence of events. Anyway, the upshot of the whole crazy thing was that Prince Zarkon— or the man I have chosen, rather melodramatically, to *call* Prince Zarkon—was in my debt to the extent of one personal favor. It has taken me three years of steady plugging away, pulling every string within my reach to pull, to persuade this amazing individual to repay me in this manner: by opening some of the less-sensitive files of Omega and by granting me interviews.

He has trusted me to be faithful to my promise to reveal or let slip nothing that might enable the curious reader to trace him to his lair. I sincerely believe that I have not betrayed that trust.

—LIN CARTER

Hollis, Long Island, New York

Chapter 1

The Hand of Death

The slopes of Mount Shasta were drenched in purple shadows, but already the first few level shafts of dawn were striking the mountain's peak with rose-and-golden fire.

The scene was a spectacular one from the ledge on the upper slope. The vista that fell away to every side was one of wild and rugged grandeur. But to the small group of five men who huddled together where the ledge widened out, their minds were on subjects other than the beauties of nature.

For the most part they waited in silence. When they did speak among themselves or address each other, it was to exchange only a few terse words, and these in a low mutter.

They were curiously dressed, the five men who waited on the mountain. Each of them was robed in a voluminous, wide-sleeved robe the precise scarlet of human blood. To these robes hodded cowls were attached, and these were drawn up as if to conceal their faces.

What little could be glimpsed of the features of the five red-robed men conveyed the impression of tension, excitement, and even apprehension. But it was hard to make out anything more, so closely were their hoods drawn, enshadowing their features.

The fifth man regretted that, for reasons of his own, which will become apparent before long. He was younger than the rest, his face tanned, healthy, alert, candid. The other men with him on the mountain were sallow, hard-bitten, with furtive eyes and twisted, cynical mouths.

From time to time, one of the five men would move uneasily, shuffle his feet, clear his throat, or cough. This waiting was beginning to get on their nerves: it always did; perhaps that is why they had been commanded to arrive early.

By now it was truly dawn.

The five men in the blood-colored robes grew tenser. No longer did they shift their weight uneasily from one foot to the other, exchange a low mutter with a comrade, or cough. They stared with a peculiar intensity at a spot on the path above them as if, for some reason, that innocent stretch of naked stone fascinated them. Beyond it, the ledge rose to curve around the wall of the mountain and vanish from sight.

As yet, the upper ledge was empty; soon it would be occupied, they knew.

They were awaiting the coming of a man, their leader, their Master. If, that is, he was in truth only a man. They worshiped yet feared him. Before he had come into their lives they had, most of them, been small-time criminals after an easy buck. Then he had come to open up vast, glittering, imperial vistas before them, to promise them power undreamed of, and strange wisdom beyond the knowledge of the sages. But he exacted a fearful price for those gifts of power and wisdom. There was only one penalty for disloyalty or failure or betrayal. That penalty was . . . *death*.

Death that struck suddenly and silently, and passed on, leaving no mark upon its victim and no sign of its passage.

There could be no hope of committing any of these sins against the Master; for the ancient wisdom of the Lemurians had bequeathed unto him the uncanny ability to read the minds of others. Or so, at least, he claimed.

The suspense became almost unendurable.

They had been instructed to gather in this weird and awful place of naked stone and windswept heights in the hour before dawn. And now, at any moment, the Master should appear among them —suddenly, without warning, from some secret place they could never ascertain.

The time was—*now*.

Suddenly the golden rays of the morning sun struck about them, driving back the shadows and blinding them momentarily with its bright dazzle. When their vision cleared, they were no longer five in number, for the Master stood before them on the ledge of rock that curved away around the side of the mountain, going nowhere.

An involuntary gasp broke from their lips, and as one man they rose to their feet to give homage to the great sage whose mighty brain contained the innermost secrets of lost and legended Lemuria.

He was a tall man, and powerfully built, with a deep chest, long arms and legs, and his heavily muscled, virile torso was wrapped from head to foot in a loose robe that was flame-crimson. He stood without moving, and it was as if he had melted into being from out of thin air and onto the ledge.

In a deep voice of resonant timbre he named

them one by one, and in response each of the five disciples lifted his right arm in salute.

"Brother Nergal, Brother Beelzebub, Brother Loki, Brother Pluto, Brother Ahriman," he said, nodding in reply to the salute of each lifted arm.

It was the whim of the Master to bestow upon each of his chief lieutenants the name of one of the gods of death and darkness and the underworld, drawn from the world's chief mythologies. No one knew why, nor dared to ask.

The man he had addressed as Brother Ahriman was the last to be named because he was the most recent member of their ranks, having been recruited by Brother Nergal only months before. When Brother Ahriman raised his right arm to salute the Master he held it aloft just a moment or two longer than might seem necessary. If the Master noticed this, he said nothing about it, and not the slightest flicker of expression crossed his powerful features to suggest that he thought anything of it.

It would take ears far more sensitive than those possessed by any human to have heard the faint clicks as the miniature camera strapped to the underside of Brother Ahriman's right arm recorded the face of the Master on supersensitive film.

With a stately gesture, the Master bade his five red-clothed underlings seat themselves. They sank to their knees while he remained standing, towering above them.

"I observe that Brother Shaitan and Brother Dis are not with us this morning," said the Master in a deep, resonant voice.

The senior member of the group—whose true name was often a matter of discussion when FBI bureau chiefs got together for shop talk, and whose sallow, unhealthy, vicious-eyed features were exhibited prominently on the bulletin boards of post offices around the country—cleared his throat timidly and made reply.

"No, Master," he said. "Brother Shaitan is occupied with a mission of whose nature I believe you have been privately informed by him."

The Master nodded grimly, saying nothing.

"And Brother Dis is in Las Vegas recruiting a number of men to make up Group 3," he concluded.

"Very well, then," said the Master. "I believe we are ready to begin."

His stance was regal, the proud lift of his bullet head imperial, as he loomed above them there on the high part of the ledge, silhouetted against the rugged and impressive grandeur of the mountain range, the wind-torn clouds of the sky behind the mountains, and the brilliance and glory of the sunrise that lit up the world.

The ceremony, which Ahriman had observed twice before, was ready to begin.

"Na kadish iom-thaa kadishtu," he intoned in ritual blessing. The language was supposedly in the lost tongue of the Lemurians, but Brother Ahriman, at least, had his doubts. Privately, he considered it to be mere gibberish.

One by one the disciples were commanded to report on the activities over which they had charge. The catalog of felonies thus reported would have delighted the heart of the district attorney of Los Angeles County, had he been fortunate enough to have been present. Rich men dying of incurable ailments and superstitious millionaires' widows with a penchant for the occult had been approached on behalf of the Brotherhood and had been promised miracle cures and fantastic secrets in return for substantial donations. A police agent on the bunco squad, who had penetrated one of their meetings, had met with a fatal accident, as had two newspaper reporters before him. The managing editor of a powerful Los Angeles newspaper, about to launch an anticultist crusade against several occult groups in general and the Brotherhood of Lemurian Wisdom in particular, had received a certain "warning" and had abruptly changed his plans.

To all of these things, Brother Ahriman listened intently.

He was the last to whom the Master turned for his report. His report was brief and succinct, his activities as yet being merely nominal—a simple matter of monitoring the many occult newsletters and underground magazines for any reference to the activities of the Brotherhood. Two of these publications in particular, he said, were loudly voicing their suspicions as to the validity of the claims of the Brotherhood. These publications were *The Rowan Tree,* a bimonthly magazine reproduced by photo-offset, edited and published by one Homer T. Breedlove of the small community of Jackson Center, and the *Borderlands Report,* a mimeographed newsletter edited and published by a young woman who lived in Palma Laguna and whose name was Elvira Higgins.

Brother Ahriman had met both of these individuals in an attempt to persuade them to subdue or suspend their criticisms of the Brotherhood. Homer T. Breedlove, a nervous rabbity little man, had proved easily intimidated, and henceforth the Brotherhood could expect at most a lukewarm press in his publication. But as for Elvira Higgins, the girl had demonstrated that she was made of sterner stuff. Not only had she refused to be cowed by

thinly veiled threats of reprisals and sanctions, but,
he reported, stifling a grin, the obstinate young
lady had driven him out of her apartment at the
point of a gun.

And not a pearl-handled "ladies' special" either,
Brother Ahriman reported, but an old-fashioned
horse pistol, a six-shooter such as had tamed the
West in the hands of stalwarts like Wyatt Earp and
Doc Holliday. This piece of portable artillery, Elvira Higgins had stoutly and significantly pointed
out, had belonged to her grandfather, a deputy
sheriff in Comanche County. "More than one big-
talking desperado had been laid low by Grandpappy's hoss pistol," she had informed him ominously. Looking at the huge weapon, Ahriman had
believed her.

Completing his report, Brother Ahriman remained standing while the Master commended him.

"It is admirable that one as yet a neophyte to our
ranks should prove so scrupulous in his duties!"
the Master said, smiling slightly. And with those
words he extended one hand in benediction, permitting his outstretched fingers to touch for just a moment the bowed head of the newest disciple. A
murmur of approval ran around the circle.

The Master raised his hand from Brother Ahriman and turned his piercing gaze upon the others.
Those eyes were strange, almost frightening in their
intensity. In color, they were virtually unique, for
they were as pale as ice, and all but colorless. In
the face of another, lesser man, they might have
seemed vague, watery, ineffectual. But not in the
face of the Master: that visage was a grim, frowning mask that radiated power, strength, and authority. Indomitable will could be read in that
iron jaw, and superhuman intelligence in the bald

brow of that bullet head. It was, quite literally, the face of a man born with the intellectual genius of a Newton and with the iron will and leadership of a Napoleon.

But there were other qualities that Brother Ahriman could read in those cold, commanding eyes, those thin, hard lips, that brutal and muscular face.

And they were the cunning of the Devil, the cruelty of a fiend, the ruthlessness of another Hitler.

The last report delivered, the Master now gave his instructions to each disciple. The lodges, or local branches of the Brotherhood, were to strive to increase their total membership through intensive advertising and recruitment measures. The beguilement of the wealthy and the superstitious was to continue with redoubled vigor. A close watch was to be maintained upon the activities of the Los Angeles editor to ascertain whether or not his yielding to their persuasion had been sincere or feigned. If he attempted to contact members of the district attorney's office, the police force, or the federal authorities, it was to be reported instantly in the usual manner—a coded advertisement in the personal columns of the Los Angeles *Illustrated Press*. Ironically, this was the very newspaper of which he was the editor!

There were other instructions. Forthcoming issues of the two occult publications were to be closely monitored; *The Rowan Tree* would probably cause no difficulty from now on, but if Elvira Higgins proved recalcitrant, the same "warning" that had seemingly converted the managing editor of the *Illustrated Press* was to be given her.

The reports made, the new instructions given, it was time to go. Yet the disciples lingered, awaiting their dismissal. The Master stood, towering above them, aloof and impassive and immobile as a statue, with a curious hint of expression in his eyes of icy flame. Was it sorrow, regret—suffering? It was hard to tell.

Then he began to speak, and now the deep organlike tones of his voice were muted and somber as if laden with melancholy.

"It has been given unto me by Those we serve to know that one amongst you has betrayed my trust," he said. As if thunderstruck, the disciples froze, then burst into a clamor of protestation and inquiry, which the Master stilled with a lifted palm.

"Silence! The Children of the Fire-Mist, who, in the Beginning, molded life upon this Earth and taught Their secret wisdom to the ancient sages of Lemuria, speak to me in the stilly watches of the night when I am at my prayers, in vigil before the altar of the Ancient Flame. The secrets of men's hearts and minds are open to Their scrutiny, nor can any hide from Their vengeance. If there truly be a Judas among us, They shall strike him down in Their own time. The invisible flames of the Fire-Mist shall enfold him and he shall die the miserable death of a traitor, accursed alike in this life and in the Second World! Now begone, all of you, that I may return to my sorrowful meditations."

They turned and went down the twisting path, leaving him in solitary thought above.

When next they turned to look, he was gone. It was as if the Master had dissolved back into the thin air from which he had materialized, for they knew, all of them, that there was no way down from that rocky ledge other than by the path on which they stood.

Chapter 2

Invisible Flames

The telephone in the glass-enclosed cubicle rang deafeningly. The tall, skinny man with the nervous eyebrows, who had been stretched out in the swivel chair rapidly scanning column after column of newsprint still fresh from the composing room, jumped three inches in the air. He came down simultaneously cursing a blue streak and hunting frantically for the phone, which was buried beneath the clutter atop his desk.

Finding the instrument and fitting it to his ear, he bellowed "Halleck!" into the mouthpiece. In the next moment he relaxed, for the voice at the other end of the line was that of his boss, Robert Russell Ryan, millionaire owner and publisher of the *Illustrated Press.*

"That you, chief? I thought it was MacAndrews, reporting back from . . . no, nothing yet on that. Sure, I gave him the minicamera and showed him how to use it. With any luck, we should have a decent picture of the devil-in-chief by this afternoon, at the latest. That's right, they're waiting right now; the darkroom's all set up, and I got Hennessey standing by the teleprinter to shoot it off to Washington for identification the minute the print's

dry. . . . Dang right I'll let you know! . . .
Okay, okay. Yeah; I'm a little jumpy too . . . this
thing's got me on edge, my nerves are crawlin' like
ninety-nine cockroaches closin' in on a chocolate
cream pie. . . . Right; will do."

Hanging the receiver back on the hook, Halleck
sat back and mopped his brow with a huge red
bandanna handkerchief. His eyebrows, thick and
furry as two fat caterpillars, crawled and wriggled
up and down his brow. He went back to reading
newsprint.

It did not even begin to happen until they reached
the rocky foot of Mount Shasta. And, once begun,
it was all over within seconds.

This was desolate country, here at the northern
extremity of the Sierra Nevada Mountains. Dirt
roads cut through scrub pine forest to join the main
highway. But here, at the base of the mysterious
mountain, there was nothing to be seen but mounds
of broken rock, tumbled slabs, and heaps of rub-
ble, partly overgrown by wiry bushes.

They came down in single file, with Brother
Ahriman the last to descend. Since he had been
walking behind the others and was thus unseen by
them, he had rolled back the sleeve of his red robes,
unstrapped the tiny camera from beneath his right
forearm, and held it hidden in his palm. In a few
moments they would remove their robes and bundle
them away, each disciple seeking his car where it
was hidden among the trees. Ahriman did not want
the camera to be seen when he unrobed in the full
view of the others.

But he never unrobed.

Suddenly, he voiced an ear-splitting scream of
pain. It was the sort of throat-ripping cry that might

be wrenched from a man if his entire body were suddenly plunged into a bath of hissing acid. None of the other men had ever heard so hideous a shriek in all their lives. They gasped, paled, and whipped around to see what had wrung such a cry from their comrade.

Ahriman, his face white as salt, his eyes virtually bulging from their sockets, stood on his tiptoes, his body bent backward in a rigid arc eloquent of unbelievable agony.

His mouth was open, the lips drawn back in a ghastly skull-like grin that bared his teeth to the gums.

For a moment only he stood thus; then he threw himself to the ground and rolled over and over in the gritty sand, rubbing his body against the earth desperately. A cold chill went through the other men as they stood there stiffly, staring at his weird contortions with wide, frightened eyes.

He acted like a man whose body was enveloped in flames and who is trying to crush the flames out against the earth. But they could see no flames, nor did his scarlet robes blacken, nor his flesh crisp. It was as if their brother was bathed in *invisible flames*. . . .

The same thought struck home to each man in the same instant. But it was he whom the Master had called Brother Nergal who was the one to give it voice.

"The Fire-Mist!" he croaked through dry lips. The others stared at him in speechless horror, then back at the writhing, mindless thing that had, only a moment before, been a man. Then, in a single concerted rush, they broke and ran for the trees where their cars were waiting. No one wanted to be left alone with the hapless traitor who had incurred

the wrath of the Master and of Those whom he
served.

In moments they were gone. And there was
nothing there at the bleak foot of Shasta except the
gasping, struggling thing that sobbed out the last
instants of its life in frightful agony.

But just before he died, a semblance of sanity
returned to Ahriman's pain-wracked mind. A
brief moment of lucidity between twin eternities of
torment. And in that moment he staggered somehow to his feet and shoved into a crevice in the rocky
wall the tiny instrument he still held clenched in his
left fist—the camera containing the film whereon
was recorded the features of the Master.

With shaking hands he shoved it deep into the
crack and plugged it with bits of broken rock.

Then he died.

The publisher of the Los Angeles *Illustrated Press,*
Mr. Robert Russell Ryan, was cooling off with a
brisk rubdown and a cold martini after an hour on
the tennis court when the telephone rang.

The voice at the other end was so distorted with
fear and a peculiar quality that Ryan knew was anger that it was a moment or two before he could
recognize it as that of Gordon Halleck, the managing editor of his Los Angeles paper.

The message Halleck imparted in a voice shaking
with rage and fright was enough to make Ryan drop
his martini glass from suddenly nerveless fingers.
His strong, intelligent face went pale to the lips.
He sat hunched over the telephone intently, drink-
ing in every word. The expression that his features
bore was curious, almost indescribable. Anger was
written there, and an odd sort of belligerence, and
legible in his lean, aristocratic features as well was
an emotion that could almost be labeled grim vin-

dication—the expression a man might wear whose direct prediction has proven accurate.

"I *knew* something like this might happen, Halleck," he almost snarled into the receiver. "Blast it all, man, you should never have gone ahead with this crazy scheme of letting one of our ace reporters infiltrate so dangerous a cult! If you had only consulted me, before sending MacAndrews in . . ."

Then, regaining control, he began to think calmly and lucidly what should next be done, ignoring the voice at the other end that attempted to justify itself. Cutting the editor's words off with a peremptory bark, Robert Russell Ryan issued three commands in a tense, hard-bitten tone of voice, and hung up on a flow of further protestations.

But he did not go back to the massage table. He was too jumpy, too nerved up, to be able to relax and enjoy the pummeling of those strong, knowing hands. Thoughts and plans, schemes and counterschemes went boiling through his brain. He muttered and grumbled under his breath, clenching and unclenching his fists. Then he poured himself another martini, an even stiffer one than before, and drank it down as if it had been orange juice.

The color had come back into his face by this time, but he was still shaken by a trembling and devouring anger similar to that which had quivered in the voice of his managing editor.

A county sheriff, acting upon an anonymous phone call, had found the corpse of a dead man, wearing curious scarlet robes, among the rocks at the base of one of the Sierra Nevada Mountains. A wallet, found in the pocket of the trousers he had been wearing under the robes at the time of his death, identified him as Horton

Anderson of Los Angeles. The same identification cards also gave his street address. A routine search of his apartment disclosed a sealed envelope marked *To be opened in the event of my death.*

Therein the sheriff found a press card identifying Horton Anderson as none other than the famous crime-busting investigative reporter, Norwell MacAndrews of the *Illustrated Press.* A note attached thereto instructed the finder to call Gordon Halleck at once.

The county sheriff, a man named Biggs, was a beefy, truculent, surly individual with no particular love for newspaper reporters. But he was smart enough to recognize MacAndrews' name instantly. At the youthful age of twenty-seven, this particular reporter had three times earned the Pulitzer Prize for journalism, and was one of the most respected names in his profession. And, as it happened, one of those three prize-winning cases had involved police corruption. A crooked police commissioner had narrowly escaped punishment, placing the blame, as well as some cleverly contrived circumstantial evidence, on a certain county sheriff named Biggs. Had it not been for the bold and daring undercover investigations of MacAndrews, Biggs would even now be spending the better part of twenty years in the state penitentiary.

Biggs swore feelingly and with surprising eloquence for five minutes straight. Then, although it ran counter to the discipline of his service, he sat down at the telephone and placed a call to Gordon Halleck, he of the nervous eyebrows.

It was the least thing Sheriff Biggs could do, to obey without question the last wishes of the daring and courageous young reporter who had saved him from disgrace and imprisonment. He did it gladly.

Almost as gladly as he would have put the cuffs on the man who had murdered Norwell Mac-Andrews.

About halfway through his second martini, Robert Russell Ryan succeeded in getting his breath back and regaining his usual clarity of mind. He thought back over the three instructions he had given Gordon Halleck.

The first of these was to search the apartment MacAndrews had taken under an assumed name, in order to secure any notes the reporter had made on the case he had been investigating at the time of his murder, before these same documents were stolen or destroyed by his murderers. This Halleck swore to do; he was, in fact, already on his way to MacAndrews' apartment at that very moment.

The second thing was to see that his body was given the most thorough autopsy money could buy, even if it meant flying in a planeful of specialists from the state medical school, placing these distinguished doctors temporarily on the payroll of the Ryan Newspaper Corporation as medical consultants.

That would cost him a bundle, he knew. But the pricetag was unimportant, he had said sternly to Halleck.

And the third of his instructions had concerned the manner in which his Los Angeles newspaper was to treat the murder of one of its own star reporters. He had commanded Gordon Halleck to work a coverup at his end—to report that an unidentified man's body had been found, death seemingly from natural causes, to print no picture of the corpse, and to bury this particular news item on the interior pages. On no account was Mac-

Andrews' true identity to be disclosed. Later on it
would be done, and with a full obituary. But for
now, let it suffice that an unidentified man had died,
and leave it at that. It was still possible that the
powers who controlled the Lemurian cult Mac-
Andrews had been trying to uncover did not know
either his real identity or his affiliations with the
newspaper.

Ryan, of course, knew of the "warning" Gordon
Halleck had received after announcing his anti-
occult crusade. It had been the uncanny nature of
that warning that had alerted Halleck to the depth
of iniquity that the cult would stoop. Ostensibly
knuckling under to thinly veiled threats upon instructions from his boss, Halleck had pretended to
have been successfully intimidated by the red-robed
devils. Actually, of course, he had assigned his ace
investigative reporter the job of digging into the cult.

A job that had resulted in the young man's
death. . . .

Robert Russell Ryan growled a sulphurous oath,
his blue eyes blazing. It was sickening enough to
know that because of him a fine young man with
a brilliant career had gone down to a miserable
death. But if the secret cultists who had contrived
his murder had any inkling of the fact that Halleck
had not been intimidated, and that Halleck stood
behind MacAndrews, there would be hell to pay.

Ryan gnawed his underlip, miserably.

He didn't want another man's death on his con-
science. Specifically, the death of his editor and
lifelong friend, Gordon Halleck!

But what more could he do, that he had not
already done?

Chewing on his lip, he stared unseeingly across
the room. There, covering the farther wall, a photo-

mural of a great eastern metropolis flung its world-famous skyscrapers against the sky. There, on that narrow island between the Hudson River and the East River, lived the one man alive on earth today who just might be able to help Ryan protect the life of his managing editor and avenge the cruel murder of his star reporter.

He picked up the phone and dialed long distance. With the speed of light itself, his call went flashing across the country, into the central switchboards of the greatest and wealthiest metropolis of the many that adorned the Eastern Seaboard, Knickerbocker City itself.

At the other end, a telephone rang. A moment later the receiver was picked up and a deep, quiet voice answered.

"This is Robert Russell Ryan, calling from California," said the wealthy publisher. "If it is humanly possible, I should like to speak to Prince Zarkon."

"Is it very important?" inquired the voice at the other end.

Robert Russell Ryan drew in a long breath and released it slowly, fighting to control his nerves.

"It is a matter of life and death," he said unsteadily.

"Then I am Prince Zarkon," replied the voice at the other end.

Chapter 3

The Omega Men

On the Upper West Side of Knickerbocker City, facing the river, there stands a certain block of ordinary-looking brownstone residence buildings. There is nothing about them in particular to attract the eye of the casual passer-by. Battered ashcans are piled beside the front steps; lace-curtained windows with discreetly drawn shades stare blankly out on the street; the rooftops are crowded with television antennae and chimneys.

Along the housefronts, geraniums bloom in window boxes. The paint is peeling from the front doors, which march in a row the length of the block. Children have scrawled the sidewalks with graffiti, and the black asphalt of the street is marked out in numbered squares for games of hopscotch. In every detail but one the block is virtually identical with hundreds of other residential neighborhoods in the giant metropolis.

And that single note of difference is small, unobtrusive, easily overlooked. It is nothing more than a small, polished brass plate set into the wall beside one of the doors midway down the block—a plate bearing only the Greek letter *omega* (Ω), which signifies The End, and also The Ultimate.

The street has few pedestrians, for it bears no shops or food stores and goes nowhere, ending at the river itself. And if any of the few who do pass by chance to notice the sign, it would be reasonable to expect them to think nothing of it. The sign could easily denote that the building houses a chapter of one of those national college fraternities whose names are Greek letters.

Only a handful of highly placed city officials and federal agents are aware that this block of innocent and seemingly ordinary buildingfronts form but a thin façade, a mask behind which lies concealed a mystery that has been penetrated by only a few.

For behind this everyday façade is a single supermodern building, occupying the entire block, completely air-conditioned and with its own private source of power.

This block-sized building is the secret head-quarters of the Omega organization, one of the smallest and least known but most powerful crime-fighting agencies in the world. An organization so small that it is composed of only five men and their mysterious Master.

Behind the front door of that building to which the brass plate bearing the *omega* symbol is affixed, is concealed a fantastic fortress guarded from entry or covert surveillance by every sophisticated means know to modern technology. Most of the doors on the block cannot be opened at all, and are only false panels set against the fabric of the walls. Those walls themselves could hardly be breached with ease, for the brownstone façade hides a triple wall of battleship steel, braced to resist anything smaller than a General Sherman tank. The front door of this building and of one or two others on the block, which seem to be ordinary painted wood, are built like bank vault doors, sheathed behind a thin veneer of wood. And the windows that face the street are not made of glass but of three-inch plastic, optically polished to be perfectly transparent, but tough enough to deflect machine-gun bullets.

Beyond the door with the brass plate lies a huge living room, appointed with every civilized luxury and decorated with faultless taste. Aubusson carpets cover the polished parquet floor, and the walls are hung with rare Flemish tapestries, mahogany bookshelves lined with thousands of volumes, and a superb collection of oils by Corot, Matisse, Rubens, and Velasquez worth millions.

Five men are disposed about the large, luxurious room awaiting the arrival of the sixth, who is their Master.

Pacing the carpet is a small, trimly built, peppery-tempered little fellow named Scorchy Muldoon. One look at his snub nose and broad upper lip, and eyes as blue as the lakes of Killarney under a thatch of fiery red, and you would have known him for an Irishman born and bred. Aloysius Murphy Muldoon was his full name; once he had been a champion bantamweight boxer famed for the speed of his fists, which fairly "scorched" the air, hence his nickname, coined by an admiring sportswriter. But that was years ago; Scorchy Muldoon had lost his temper in the ring, killing his opponent with the fury of his blows. Such accidents do occur in prize fights, but Scorchy, unable to forget that he had murdered a man, sought refuge in the bottle. In a whiskey-soaked haze he threw over his promising career and slid into the gutter, from which a strong hand had rescued him—the

hand of the Master of Fate, whom he now lives
only to serve.

Stretched out on a sofa is the lanky length of a
gentleman with the pointed goatee, waxed mustachios, and arched ironic brows of Mephisto himself.
His shallow skin, blue-black hair, and air of lazy,
amused mockery lend him a curiously theatrical
appearance, enhanced by his narrow pinstripe suit
and natty gloves. He is Nick Naldini, master of
sleight-of-hand, a former stage magician and escape
artist who trod the boards of five continents as
Mephisto the Marvelous. The tragic death of his
wife and babe had plunged the mercurial Mephisto
into a black depression, from which he found his
only surcease in the deathly white powder called
cocaine. His stage career wrecked, he turned to
gambling with crooked cards, for those supple,
long-fingered hands could stack a deck as easily as
they could pick a pocket or crack a safe. From the
slow death of cocaine as from a life of sordid
crime, he had been saved by the strong hand of the
Man of Mysteries to whom he has now dedicated
the rest of his life.

Sprawled in an easy chair sits a tanned, frank,
open-faced former crack test pilot and air ace,
Francis "Ace" Harrigan. He downed forty enemy
planes over Indochina, but a too-eager hand on
the firing button had slain a novice airman of his
squadron who happened to be the younger brother
of the girl Harrigan loved with all his heart.
Cashiered from the service, returned home, unable
to bear the horror and loathing in her eyes, his
reason cracked. From the very brink of suicide he
had been salvaged by the wise counsels of the
Lord of the Unknown, whom he now serves with
all his ability.

At a Chippendale desk in the corner, flipping rapidly through a volume of facts and figures whose twelve hundred pages he could commit to memory in less than ten minutes, sits a huge, hulking, oafish-looking fellow with outsized feet and pale, freckled hands as big as boxing gloves, named Theophilus "Doc" Jenkins. With his heavy-jawed face, watery blue eyes, and wispy, colorless hair, he resembles an amiable halfwit. Few men would guess that behind his heavy-fleshed, dull-eyed visage is one of the most remarkable human brains in existence—for this man has the rare ability to remember instantly any face he has ever seen, any voice he has ever heard, any page he has ever scanned. The man with the camera eyes and the computer brain had been condemned to a mental asylum until redeemed by the wisdom of the Lord of the Unknown, whom he now calls Master.

Hunched over a sheaf of electronic diagrams, a skinny, frail little man sits in the corner, sharp peevish eyes in his waspish face intently fixed on the rapid scribblings of his pen. His arms and legs are so thin and fragile he looks as if you could snap him in two with your bare hands; however, the man rash enough to try would find himself being tied in painful knots by a wiry-muscled master of kung fu and karate. Few would recognize this skinny scarecrow for the scientific genius Mendel Lowell "Menlo" Parker, who had been a wizard of electrical science, the peer of Tesla or Marconi, until struck down by a dread, wasting disease. From this incurable illness Menlo Parker had been cured by the surgical skills of the Ultimate Man at whose service he has placed all the resources of his brilliant intellect.

These five men, and the Master they love and

serve with all the loyalty of their grateful hearts, comprise the Omega organization, which is dedicated to the destruction of those super-criminals who employ the clever tricks of modern science to prey upon the superstitious fears of the common man.

Scorchy Muldoon was getting restless. The peppery little bantamweight could rarely sit still for long, and was never so happy as when he was venturing into danger or wading into a fight.

"What's keeping the chief?" he grumbled, pacing like a caged tiger. "He told us to be here by two; it's now quarter past."

"Relax; take it easy," drawled Nick Naldini from his languid position on the sofa. "If he said he'd be here, he'll be here. Anybody know what's up?"

Menlo Parker cleared his throat, putting down his sheaf of diagrams and peering across them to where the magician lay sprawled lazily. "I have no idea, Nicholas, but the chief got a call from the Coast about noontime. From California, I think. Someone named Ryan—"

"Newspaper publisher," rumbled Doc Jenkins from the desk in the corner. "A man of considerable wealth and influence in Los Angeles, I believe."

"You 'believe,' is it, me bucko?" grinned Scorchy Muldoon. "Don't be after pullin' our leg, you big galoot! You could probably reel off his holdings to the last penny, and quote his Social Security number to boot." The big, heavy-jawed man with the stupid-looking face grinned at him amiably, and shuffled his Size 14s embarrassedly.

"Here's the chief now," observed Ace Harrigan alertly. They turned to greet their Master.

The man who now entered the room from his secret sanctum beneath the city greeted them with a nod. To the eye he seemed an ordinary-looking figure. At a couple of inches over six feet, he was only a trifle above the average height. Although his body was superbly muscled—was, in fact, one of the most perfectly developed physiques in the world with a symmetrical build and evenly developed musculature—he seemed nothing more than a healthy, athletically inclined man of perhaps thirty.

It was only at second or third glance that you found something about him that arrested your attention. Perhaps it was the strange, tawny shade of his skin, which was not precisely that of an Oriental, but seemed more Polynesian than anything else. Or it could have been the classic regularity of his features, which were handsome without seeming effeminate, and whose impassive and majestic immobility was like a mask. Scorchy Muldoon often thought, irreverently, that his chief would have made a great poker player with that face, if the Ultimate Man ever cared to indulge in such frivolous forms of entertainment.

The attention of most who saw the chief was drawn at once to the breadth of his nobly proportioned brow, which denoted a highly developed brain many times superior to the most brilliant intellects of which the planet could boast. Either that, or his eyes were likely to seize and hold your fascinated gaze. These last were truly striking. Large, deeply set, and wide apart under that towering brow, they were orbs of scintillant, intense, jet-black magnetic fire. Those eyes could virtually hypnotize at a glance. Indeed, so hypnotic were they that their possessor commonly concealed them behind sunglasses when in public for just that reason.

He was neatly but oddly dressed in a turtle-neck pullover made of stretch fabric in gun-metal gray. Gray, too, was the supple suede jacket and slacks he wore. His shoes were also of gray suede, a color which, for some peculiar reason, he seemed to favor inordinately. His hair was of the same precise shade, sleek and heavy and smooth, with locks arranged across his brow in a fashion reminiscent of some of the ancient Roman portrait busts in the International Museum. Few beyond his five lieutenants knew that he was completely bald and that the pewter-toned hairpiece was false.

The reason behind this omnipresent gray monotone of dress was a complexly psychological one. Whenever he appeared in public, it was in this fashion. So distinct and unique an appearance did he present, for this reason, that people tended to think of him in this manner. That made a matter of personal disguise, whenever he chose to employ one, all the more effective.

And besides, this one was one of his "business suits," as it amused Scorchy Muldoon and the others to think of them. Probably only a fully equipped police lab, with a couple of weeks at their disposal, could have discovered all the special gimmicks and gadgets cunningly concealed in what seemed at first and even at second glance to be an ordinary suit of clothing.

In a lifetime filled with suspense and peril and danger, he had seen it proved many times that the advantage of surprise can often carry the day against even overwhelming odds. For that reason, the Man of Mysteries took every precaution his brilliant mind could envision to protect himself and those who fought beside him in the unending war between supercrime and civilization.

Such a man was Zarkon, Lord of the Unknown,

who addressed them now in quiet, vibrant tones that bore the steely ring of command.

"I called you together for a mission," he said into the intent silence of the room. "In California, a man has been killed by a mysterious force. He was a good man, honest and intelligent, and devoted to uncovering crime in high places. Another man has asked for our assistance in exposing his killer and in rooting out what may be a secret criminal conspiracy. He, too, is a good man—a man of influence, wealth, and power who uses these faculties to crusade for good government and to search out criminality. We are going to his aid this afternoon. We will take the *Shooting Star* and equipment cases 9, 11, and 14."

Scorchy Muldoon was the first of them all to break the silence.

"Oboyoboyoboy!" he grinned, blue eyes sparkling with anticipation. "It's about time, too! I been spoilin' for a good, hot brawl for ever so long."

Prince Zarkon said nothing. But he had a feeling that, before long, the peppery little prize fighter would have his wish.

Chapter 4

The Secret Brotherhood

The five men and their Master, together with their fighting gear and the equipment cases that Zarkon had specified, descended by an elevator into the sublevels of their headquarters. There a pneumatic tube carried them swiftly and secretly under the Henry Hudson River to a small private island midway between Knickerbocker City and the rocky cliffs of New Jersey.

Omega Island was so small it was found only on U. S. Department of the Interior geological survey maps. The entire island was the personal property of Prince Zarkon, and was protected from city, state, and federal interference because it was under the diplomatic immunity of the flag of Novenia, a small Balkan republic of which until recently Prince Zarkon had been ruler.

From the air, the small island appeared deserted save for some dilapidated shacks of corrugated iron and a rickety boat dock. Most of the Omega facilities were underground or concealed by clever camouflage. It was here that the Omega men kept their private planes and boats, among which were a luxurious yacht that packed the gunpower of a pocket battleship, one of the most powerful privately

39

owned submarines in the world, and a variety of speedboats and aircraft.

The underwater pneumatic tube debouched before another elevator, which took them to the surface. While Ace Harrigan prepared Zarkon's private jet, the *Shooting Star,* for the flight, the other men loaded aboard their gear and equipment. Before very long they were ready for the takeoff.

The island was too small to have room for a regular runway such as are used by ordinary jet aircraft. But, then, the *Shooting Star* was not an ordinary plane. Zarkon had modified the design with a few improvements of his own, among which was a bank of rocket tubes that permitted the craft to take off almost vertically.

They strapped themselves into seats with inflated pneumatic cushions, fitted with hydraulic gear that absorbed most of the brutal thrust of the rocket tubes. With Ace Harrigan at the controls, the *Shooting Star* went soaring up from Omega Island and ascended to about twenty-six thousand feet. Leveling off at the altitude of five miles, the speedy little craft arrowed across the continent at a velocity that would have impressed the pilots of conventional jetcraft.

Once the flight was under way, Zarkon and his lieutenants unstrapped themselves and set to work. The Omega organization seldom went into action without advance preparations, which included the amassing of as much relevant information as could be assembled. Zarkon swiftly briefed his men on the situation. Radiophones were built into the cabin by each seat, and while Nick Naldini inquired into the ownership, structure, and affairs of the secret occult Brotherhood the murdered reporter had been investigating, the others did similar research, quickly compiling dossiers of relevant information on all individuals thus far known to be connected with the case. By early afternoon they began to make their reports to Zarkon.

Ryan's wealth was sizable and entirely accounted for by the success of his newspaper empire; no law-enforcement official from the U. S. Attorney General to the Los Angeles district attorney had any reason to suspect him of surreptitious or criminal activities.

"But, cripes, we knew that already," grouched Scorchy Muldoon under his breath to Nick Naldini. "I mean, heck, isn't he the guy we're goin' out to help?"

"Maybe so, boy," drawled the former magician sardonically. "But it wouldn't be the first time the master crook behind a scheme called loudly for an investigation, just to keep out of suspicion."

As for the cult, the Los Angeles Chamber of Commerce reported that it was a legally registered religious enterprise, chartered under the corporate laws of the state, and owned by a number of individuals whose names were unfamiliar even to the computer memory of Doc Jenkins. Follow-up checks on these names with the FBI disclosed that none of them possessed criminal records—at least not under the names that appeared on the corporation papers.

The Better Business Bureau, said Menlo Parker, recorded upward of a dozen complaints against the so-called "Brotherhood of Lemurian Wisdom" that ranged from the making of fraudulent claims down to veiled attempts at monetary coercion. The Bureau, unfortunately, operated only in an advisory function and could not institute investigations. The same sort of complaints, the Bureau head reluctantly admitted, had been listed at one time or another against half the medical quacks, faith healers, phony cults, and mail-order occult schools in the state of California; they were accustomed to this sort of thing, and the situation was nothing new to them.

Both the federal authorities and the local police agencies had nothing whatsoever on Gordon Halleck, the managing editor of Robert Russell Ryan's Los Angeles paper. Halleck had worked on one or another of the several papers in the Ryan newspaper syndicate for thirty years. And as far as they knew, he was completely straight and always had been, they said, giving the editor a clean bill of health as far as their criminal files went.

The leader of the Brotherhood was a man known as Lucifer. This was the only name by which he was known to his followers, and although it was obviously a nom de plume, they had no information as to his true legal name or identity. No one knew which of the several names on the corporation papers was his.

The nearest major city to Mount Shasta was the metropolis of Palma Laguna. In an exclusive suburb of Palma Láguna known as Seagrove, Robert Russell Ryan had his country estate. There Russell màintained a private jet and his own airfield, so it was convenient for Ace Harrigan to bring the *Shooting Star* down at the private field and house it in one of the hangars. Servants on Ryan's staff unloaded their gear and escorted them to the house, a rambling estate house in the Georgian style, brick walls covered with ivy. Ryan himself met them in the study. A tall, lean, distinguished-looking man, with aristocratic features and piercing gray eyes, he

unerringly picked out their leader from among
them, although Zarkon had seldom allowed himself to be photographed.

"Prince Zarkon? Thank heaven you're here! I
really hadn't expected you this quickly, but your
rooms are being made ready now."

They shook hands. "These are my lieutenants,
Mr. Ryan. Scorchy Muldoon, Nick Naldini, Menlo
Parker, Doc Jenkins, and my pilot, Ace Harrigan."

Ryan greeted them in turn, inquired into what
they would like to drink, and invited them to choose
seats before a huge fieldstone fireplace in which
flames crackled. Zarkon got directly to the matter
at hand.

"Why was your paper investigating this cult?"
he asked.

Ryan ran the fingers of one hand through his
dark, gray-flecked hair. He frowned thoughtfully.

"Let me see, now, if I can phrase this ac-
curately," he said. "Our state is known far and
wide as a haven for cultists of the so-called lunatic
fringe. Buddhism, Vedanta, Bahai, Zen, these are
the most respectable of the religions locally represented. But we also have more than our share of
flying saucer groups, Atlantis cults, mediums, and
spiritualists, and just about anything else you can
think of."

He frowned again. "Now, for the most part, the
adherents of these fringe groups and cults are decent, honest, law-abiding citizens, sincere in their
rather exotic interests and religious beliefs, and
freely and openly exercising their constitutional
rights. *But*," he said emphasizing the word with
a lifted finger, "the occultists leave themselves peculiarly open and vulnerable to unscrupulous
hoaxers, downright charlatans, and spellbinders

who use drugs, sex, and Satanism to stir the emotions. We have a lot of elderly people who settle here for retirement in our beautiful climate. It is this kind of person, the gullible, the sick, the frightened, who are such easy prey to the occult gangster, the occult racketeer. Gordon Halleck will be here in a moment—I called him to come over when you announced your arrival by radiophone—and he can fill you in on just how big and rich and powerful the occult underworld can be, at least in potential. We feel it our duty to protect the people, even against themselves, by digging into and exposing the occult rackets, where such can be exposed. And we have plenty of reason to think this Brotherhood of Lemurian Wisdom is one of the rottenest and most unscrupulous of them all!"

When Gordon Halleck arrived, his bushy eyebrows were wriggling up his scalp, nervously. He was obviously impressed by Prince Zarkon, and avowed his eagerness to cooperate in every way with his investigations.

"I have here the coroner's report on poor Mac-Andrews," he said, handing some papers to the Ultimate Man. "And Mr. Ryan had a private team of specialists perform a very thorough and extensive autopsy on the body. Trouble is, you see, there's no known cause of death. His heart just—well—*stopped*."

"Had he any history of heart disease?" asked Zarkon.

Robert Russell Ryan spoke up. "Absolutely not! His heart was as sound as a dollar."

"How do you happen to know that?" inquired Zarkon. The publisher replied that all of his employees belonged to a company-financed health

plan as one of the fringe benefits of their employment, and that MacAndrews had been thoroughly
checked over about six weeks before his death. Zarkon checked through the coroner's report and read
the autopsy statement. It was completely negative.
No drugs or poisons or foreign substances of any
kind had been found, nor were there any wounds or
unusual marks upon the body, save for a few minor
scratches and contusions on the chest where Mac-
Andrews had seemingly for some reason rubbed
into the dirt and grit at the bottom of the mountain
path. Zarkon nodded, handed the papers to Doc
Jenkins for his scrutiny, and addressed a rapid
series of questions to Halleck.

"How did MacAndrews gain entry into the cult?"

"He permitted himself to be converted, if that's
the right word, at one of the public meetings at
their main temple in downtown Los Angeles," said
Halleck. "He donated ten thousand dollars to their
cause, his pretended savings; actually, the money
was supplied by the paper."

"How much had he reported to you before he
died?"

"Nothing concrete, just suspicions. He rose
rapidly in the hierarchy of the Brotherhood, but
until very recently was not high enough to be privy
to any of the dirty work we suspect is going on. He
was going to call me about noontime, following his
first meeting with the Circle of Disciples, convened
at dawn by this fellow they call Lucifer."

"When MacAndrews was working undercover on
a case, as he was here, was it his custom to write
his notes down or to keep them in his head?"

"Generally, he would write his information
down as he gathered it, and send it along to me
through a go-between."

"Was a go-between used in this case?" Zarkon asked. Halleck shook his head. "No. He thought that would be too dangerous."

"Yet you found no notes when you searched his flat, and he had not sent anything along to you?"

Halleck replied in the negative.

"Had anyone else searched his flat, could you tell?"

"No, just the sheriff. And he's been co-operating with us fully. MacAndrews once saved him from an undeserved jail sentence. He recognized his name on the press card he found and called me at once. He showed me everything he found, and I found nothing of interest on my own," said Halleck.

Zarkon thought intently for a moment, then addressed a new question to the editor.

"Was there ever an undercover case like this one, where MacAndrews kept notes but did not send them to you?"

Halleck started to shake his head, then blinked surprisedly and nodded. "Yes, by golly, there was! The Bryson case—remember that one, chief? Mac used to scribble his notes down and mail them to himself under a phony name at a post office box in, where was it, yeah, Yarbro City!"

Doc Jenkins shuffled his big feet and cleared his throat apologetically. At Zarkon's inquiring glance, the oafish man said: "That's a little whistle stop east of here about fifteen miles."

Zarkon nodded his thanks and asked Halleck if he could remember the number of the post office box MacAndrews had used on that occasion.

"No, I don't, but I can find out for you. We paid for the box rental, so it's in our files somewhere."

Zarkon asked him to report the number to them

here as soon as the office opened. Then he turned to Nick Naldini.

"First thing in the morning, Nick, rent a car locally and drive out to Yarbro City. Perhaps Mac-Andrews followed the same procedure in this case. At least it's worth a try."

Nick Naldini nodded affably, but a sparkle of excitement twinkled in his lazy black eyes. Scorchy Muldoon, however, pouted and eyed the lanky magician rebelliously.

"How come *he* always gets the fun, chief? It ain't fair! Sure an' I'm spoilin' for a little action meself."

Zarkon shook his head without replying, but Nick Naldini gave the peppery little boxer a leering grin.

"Because, boy, the chief doesn't wish to have you spread yourself all over the highway, taking along a couple of dozen taxpayers with you when you go," he drawled wickedly.

Scorchy Muldoon flushed, but said nothing, merely grumbling under his breath. Doc Jenkins grinned and skinny Menlo Parker cackled. It was a standing joke among the lieutenants of Zarkon that the red-headed pugilist was the worst single driver they had ever seen in their lives. What was so remarkable about this was that Scorchy Muldoon was so enormously competent in so many other areas of endeavor. He could, in a pinch, pilot a plane nearly as well as Ace Harrigan himself, and he could speak almost as many languages as could Jenkins, the man with the camera eyes and tape-recorder brain. When it came to fighting, of course, Scorchy was an undisputed whiz: He was a power-house when it came to rough-and-tumble, and could more than hold his own against the top boxers, wrestlers, judo, or kung fu experts in the world.

But when it came to driving a car, he was lucky to get a full block away from the place he started from without smashing a tail light, scratching a fender, or scaring some poor pedestrian halfway to heart failure.

As soon as Zarkon had completed his questioning of Halleck, the editor left in his own car for the lengthy drive back to Los Angeles. He had to be at the plant, he explained, in order to put the paper to bed. As soon as he had gone, Zarkon turned to the publisher.

"How well do you know this man of yours, Halleck, and how far do you trust him?" he asked.

The publisher blinked. "Why—why—I've known him for twenty years—ever since I took over control of the corporation when my father died! I would trust Gordon Halleck implicitly, with my life, if such were necessary! He's the smartest, toughest, most honest and hard-hitting man I've had in my pay, at least since Steve Wilson retired from my Chicago paper. And if you remember the days when Steve Wilson was editing the Chicago *Illustrated Press,* you know what a crime buster he was; and that should give you some idea of how high my opinion of Gordon Halleck is! Surely, Prince Zarkon, you don't for one minute think he's mixed up in this filthy business?"

Zarkon shook his head. "Not seriously," he said. "But at this stage, all I have is a lot of questions and very, very few answers. And let me remind you of one thing, Mr. Ryan: *Somebody* informed Lucifer that MacAndrews had penetrated the cult. MacAndrews was an old hand at this game of working from the inside; he would never have given himself away through a momentary slip. *Somebody* at your end must have betrayed him. . . ."

Ryan paled and bit his lip, his eyes haunted and thoughtful. The implications of Prince Zarkon's calm statement were, to say the least, shattering. And even frightful.

Chapter 5

The Hidden Camera

Not all of the newspapers in that part of California had reason to be as reticent about the MacAndrews mystery as did the *Illustrated Press,* which buried it in a small item on the inner pages.

One of the big metropolitan dailies, which specialized in old-fashioned sensationalism, played it up big on the front page, and even got a photo of the murdered man's face at the city morgue. Ramming the story through, the paper got it on the streets in time for their afternoon edition.

Among the subscribers to that particular newspaper was Miss Elvira Higgins of Palma Laguna, the editor of the *Borderlands Report.* The same Miss Elvira Higgins whose loudly phrased questioning of the validity of the Brotherhood's claims to occult knowledge had aroused the attention and might arouse in time the ire of Lucifer.

The young lady was turning the crank on her mimeograph, which was set up on her kitchen table, when the afternoon newspaper arrived on her doorstep. Opening it, her attention was immediately caught by the glaring headline that thundered in big black letters, "CULTIST SLAIN IN MYSTERY DEATH."

51

The photograph of the dead man's face, which occupied most of the remaining space on the front page, brought a gasp of amazement to the young woman's luscious, well-formed lips, for she knew the still-unidentified man, or at least she had met him. Only two days before, he had interviewed her right here in her apartment, ostensibly on the behalf of the Brotherhood. She had found him rather likable, although she had reason to heartily disapprove of the organization in which he served. And now he was dead—struck down mysteriously, and at the very base of Mount Shasta!

That last piece of information intrigued her greatly, for in recent years there had been many mysterious goings-on around that particular mountain. Curious lights had been seen flickering about the crest of the peak, and observers had been quoted in the sensationalist press as having watched through binoculars strange robed and hooded men busied about weird ceremonies upon the mountain itself on more than one occasion.

As it happened, Elvira Higgins maintained a healthy streak of skepticism in her makeup. For years she had been interested in curious events, mysterious phenomena, inexplicable mysteries. What had begun as an intellectual curiosity in college had developed into a fascinating hobby, which had led her to the collecting of reports and sightings and incidents such as this, which had in turn led to the establishment of her magazine. Mount Shasta in particular interested her: In her files there was a bulky folder stuffed with news clippings concerning the mystery mountain.

On impulse, Elvira Higgins returned to the kitchen, removed the stencil from the mimeograph, put her car keys in her purse, and took a

California road map from the kitchen drawer. She
determined to explore the death site in person.
There was not much hope that she could find a clue
the county sheriff and the metropolitan police had
missed, but she was a firm believer in psychometry
and believed that a sensitive person, such as herself, could sometimes read indications left in the
atmosphere of a place in the form of vibrations or
an astral residue.

The state highway passed near enough to the
foot of Mount Shasta for her to cover the remaining
distance on foot. And the newspaper, on its inner
pages, contained a drawing of the mountain marked
to show the exact position at which the corpse had
been found. With a little frown of determination
creasing her brows, the attractive redhead watched
the road ahead of her, her mind busied with
thoughts and speculations.

By the time her car turned off the highway and
followed a bumpy dirt road to the woods at the
foot of the mountain, the shadows of evening were
beginning to thicken.

Elvira Higgins took her flashlight from the glove
compartment, snatched up the newspaper sketch,
which she had torn from the page, and climbed out
from behind the wheel. Her high heels were not
exactly ideal footgear for such rocky and broken
terrain, but the plucky girl gritted her teeth and
made her way to the base of the mountain. By the
time she got to the spot marked with a big black
"X" on the map, she had two runs in her stockings
and had broken off one heel. But her eyes were
gleaming with excitement and her bosom heaved
with the thrill of mystery and adventure.

The place where the body had been found was,

by now, completely deserted. The police, reporters, and the crowd of sight-seers had long since gone. The position of the body on the gritty path was marked with white chalk. The girl began looking around her, alertly searching with her eyes and her mind for something—anything—that was out of the ordinary.

She found it almost at once. Why it had been overlooked by everyone else remains one of the unsolved riddles of psychology. Perhaps it was because police tend to think like police. At the scene of a murder, their minds tend to the direction of bloodstains, footprints, rifle cartridges, cigar butts. What Elvira Higgins spotted almost instantly was nothing remotely like those clues.

At about shoulder height on the mountain wall there was a small horizontal crack or crevice. It was stuffed with broken rock. In itself, there was nothing mysterious about the fact. But Elvira Higgins had studied the geology of her native state, and she knew that, while the crevice itself was in a wall of ordinary mountain granite, the rocks stuffed into it were common, ordinary ground shale.

Now, why would anybody pick up a handful of ground shale, and stuff a crevice with it?

That was the question that rose to Elvira's mind the moment her bright green eyes fastened upon the miniature mystery. The answer came almost at once.

To hide something.

Shifting the flashlight to her left hand, Elvira reached up and carefully removed the shale, piece by piece. At the back of the crevice she found something small and flat that had been hastily wedged inside.

It was a miniature camera no bigger than a box

of matches, to which an elastic strap was fastened. Her heart pounding with excitement, Elvira slipped the tiny camera into the pocket of her jacket and began to make her way back to where she had parked her car.

From a rocky ledge far above, keen, cold, hard eyes watched her every move through the lenses of a powerful pair of field glasses.

It was simplicity itself for Nick Naldini to open the lock on the post office box. As Mephisto the Marvelous, the former stage magician had often vied with his great and good friend Harry Houdini in opening locks without resorting to anything so mundane as a key. Nick wore about him at all times a slim-bladed, odd-looking instrument that could be concealed in the palm of his hand and that could open anything up to a safe with a combination lock.

He rented a car at the nearest Avis office, disguised himself as a typical tourist in a loud sports shirt and dark glasses, and entered the post office at Yarbro City during the noon hour, when post offices are most busy. Nobody paid any attention to him as he strolled with lazy slouch into the small alcove lined with post office boxes, found the one MacAndrews had used, unlocked it with a twist of the curious little instrument, took out half a dozen thick, cheap envelopes embossed with the name and the address of the residence hotel Mac-Andrews had been staying at, slipped them into his pocket, and strolled lazily back to his rented car.

He drove directly to Ryan's palatial estate in Seagrove. Zarkon and the others were just finishing their breakfast coffee when he entered with the envelopes. Opening them and scrutinizing their contents brought a chorus of groans from the five lieutenants.

"Cripes, looks like he kept his notes in some kinda Arabic!" loudly complained Scorchy Muldoon.

Doc Jenkins examined them and said in his slow, dull way that while they might look something like simplified Arabic to the untutored eye, there was no legitimate resemblance at all.

"Looks to me like some sort of private code," he said slowly. "Always thought a complete made-up language and alphabet, including invented grammar and punctuation, would make about the most unbeatable code ever devised. Seems like an awful lot of work for a reporter to go to, though. You make anything of it, chief?"

Doc Jenkins handed the notes to the Master of Fate. Behind his oafish clumsiness lurked a genuine respect, for, while he had spent years bending his amazing mental talents to the mastering of languages from Abyssinian to Zapoltopec, Zarkon was in this, as in so many other ways, his superior.

The Ultimate Man studied the closely written sheets thoughtfully, then selected from one of the many interior pockets wherewith his gray suede jacket was unobtrusively fitted a small, flat mirror of optically polished steel. He held it up so that the first sheets were reflected in the mirror, the writing appearing backward.

"It is nothing but ordinary shorthand," he said, "written backward from right to left, so that it only becomes legible when reflected in a mirror. Leonardo da Vinci was the first man to conceal his thoughts in that manner, except, of course, that he didn't write in shorthand, which was not an invention of the Italian Renaissance."

"By golly, you're right!" marveled Doc Jenkins delightedly. "Pretty darn shrewd idea." Zarkon handed the big man the notes to transcribe, and in a surprisingly short time Doc Jenkins returned, grinning hugely. The laborious process of deciphering the writing had not appealed to him, so he had simply and swiftly mastered the trick of reading shorthand in reverse.

The notes proved to be a gold mine of succinct information and clever guesswork, but contained little of any real substance. Toward the end, though, there appeared some remarks that seemed to interest Zarkon. In this section MacAndrews had discussed the occult newsletters that had been so severe in their criticism of the Brotherhood as to cause Lucifer to direct the disguised reporter to seek to squelch further such news items by intimidation of their editors.

"That seems a promising lead," Zarkon said thoughtfully. "Scorchy, why don't you look these people up and see if they have anything concrete to give us? Doc will copy out their addresses for you; you should at least be able to interview the woman in Palma Laguna who edits *Borderlands*. Report back here when you are finished with her, and we'll see about the other person later."

"Oboyoboyoboy," grinned Scorchy, rubbing his palms together briskly. "A little action, at last! Translate that gobbledegook for me, Doc, and I'm off!"

The man with the camera eyes noted down the address of Miss Elvira Higgins and handed the little Irishman the piece of paper. The boxer made a fast exit, but not fast enough to miss the perennial parting crack that Nick Naldini invariably made on such occasions.

"Take a bus, boy, or a taxi. We got enough to do
catching murderers without having to bail you out
of the clink for sixty-three traffic violations!"

Despite the advice of Nick Naldini, the feisty little
fighter took the rented car the ex-magician had
left parked before Robert Russell Ryan's estate, the
keys obligingly stuck in the ignition. It sorely
rankled Scorchy Muldoon that his driving skill was
a subject of amusement to his associates, and he
deliberately got behind the wheel of a car at every
opportunity, obviously on the theory that all a car
needs is a strong, stubborn hand at the reins in
order to know when it is licked.

The rented car, however, behaved in precisely
the usual sort of erratic manner that cars insisted
on adopting whenever the Pride of the Muldoons
got behind the wheel. Luckily, at this hour there
was hardly any traffic on the suburban streets, and
even fewer pedestrians. Thus the little bantamweight managed to reach Palma Laguna without
any of the usual mayhem and manslaughter that
generally he left in his wake.

Pulling up in front of the block of garden apart-
ments in which Elvira Higgins resided, he managed
to park without mishap. True, he narrowly missed
a red-headed matron who had injudiciously chosen
that hour to escort her toy poodle around the block
for sanitary purposes. The woman squeaked as his
fender nearly took the permanent-press crease out
of her pink slacks, snatched up her yapping pet
in shaking arms, and retired to a safe distance
behind the nearest tree.

Oblivious to this, the little boxer got out, went
up the path to the door, and rang the bell. A few
moments later his blue eyes widened and his lips

made the shape of a silent whistle, for the vision of girlish pulchritude that appeared in the doorway in no wise resembled his expectations.

From a name like Miss Elvira Higgins, Scorchy Muldoon may perhaps be forgiven for assuming that the owner of that cognomen would be a sixty-ish spinster given to wrinkle cream and Geritol. The plumply curvaceous young woman who answered the door, however, bore little semblance to his vision. Her lips were lush and sweetly curved, her eyes cool and green, her red curls deliciously tousled, the bridge of her small, adorable nose sprinkled with the cutest freckles he had seen in years. Ever susceptible to feminine charms, Scorchy was rendered speechless.

What she held, firmly gripped between two small, capable hands, didn't help his loquacity much, either.

It was an old-fashioned six-shooter so big it looked like it could blow him across the street. And it was pointed unwaveringly at his navel.

Chapter 6

The Hooded Men

Scorchy never enjoyed having guns pointed at him, even under the best of circumstances, and this wasn't one of them. The young lady had a determined glint in her eye that he profoundly disliked. He gulped, swallowed, and essayed a genial, friendly grin.

"Sure and there's no need to be after bringin' up the artillery, miss," he said weakly. In times of sudden stress his brogue came over him until he sounded like a stage Hibernian.

"Who are you and what do you want?" snapped Elvira Higgins.

He told her. Her features reflected a thorough lack of belief. Moving his hands with careful slowness, Scorchy plucked a wallet from the inside breast pocket of his loud plaid jacket and let the girl snatch it from him. The secret pocket sewn into the lining would have fooled the cleverest pickpocket, so he instructed her in how to locate it. She withdrew several folded notes, each addressed "To Whom It May Concern." The rich, embossed papers crackled as she unfolded them, keeping one suspicious eye warily on the embarrassed, grinning Irishman.

The text of the several notes was virtually identical; it identified the holder by name and formally
requested all private citizens, law-enforcement
agencies, and federal employees to render to him
any service or accommodation he might require.

It was not the text but the signatures below it
that caused the green eyes of Elvira Higgins to
widen. The signatures were from those of the state's
governor, the President of the United States himself, and the Secretary General of the United
Nations.

Together, they formed a more than adequate
testimonial to the legitimacy of Aloysius Murphy
Muldoon and his mission. The girl blushed a de-
lightful crimson and hastily tucked the enormous
six-shooter into her bag.

"I—I certainly must apologize, Mr. Muldoon,
I thought . . . well . . . you were one of the
men in the black car."

Scorchy pricked up his ears. "What car is that,
miss? And could we be after goin' inside while we
chat? 'Tis more private-like, you know."

She let him in. The ground-floor apartment was
neatly if Spartanly decorated. Bookshelves held a
small library of reference works on occultism, meta-
physics, and unexplained phenomena among which
the feisty little bantamweight recognized the works
of Charles Fort. There were also bound volumes
of the newsletter of which Elvira Higgins was editor
and publisher.

In a few brief, well-chosen words, the girl informed him of her early-evening expedition to the
foot of Mount Shasta, her discovery of the miniature camera, and of her suspicions that a long
black limousine had trailed her at least partway

home. Scorchy's Killarney-blue eyes sparkled with excitement.

"A camera, you say? Near where the body was found? Begorra, but that's the sort of thing we're lookin' for!"

The girl gestured off toward the kitchen. "I have a darkroom," she said, "because a lot of the photographs I use in *Borderlands* are my own work. I have the films developing now. I . . ." she hesitated, bit her lip, then continued, "I hope I didn't do anything wrong or break some law in developing the pictures. But I was so curious to see what the film recorded that I just went ahead and did it."

"Faith, you've nothin' to worry about on that score," Scorchy said reassuringly. "Let's see what you've got, if the pictures are ready."

She brought them out, still dampish. Scorchy began looking through them alertly.

"The filmstrip was so tiny I had to keep blowing them up," she said. "I hope I didn't lose any detail. This one of the man's face seems to be the most important, so I made several copies."

She handed them to him. Several pictures were of a number of robed and hooded men whose faces, in whole or in part, were either concealed by their garments or obscured because of the predawn lighting. But the picture of one man's face was distinct and perfectly clear. It was strong-jawed and thin-lipped, a bald bullet head with fierce eyes and an expression of command. Scorchy felt instinctively that this man was a leader, perhaps the enigmatic "Lucifer" who, according to MacAndrews' notes, was the boss of the whole occult order. He tucked the sheaf of pictures into his jacket pocket.

"You say MacAndrews interviewed you here?"

"The murdered man whose picture was in the morning paper? Yes, but his name wasn't Mac-Andrews then. Ahriman, he called himself; Brother Ahriman. He represented the Brotherhood, he said, and wanted to persuade me to refrain from publishing any more queries about the order in *Borderlands*. He was eloquent and persuasive, although I had the feeling he wasn't really very interested in getting me to lay off. He seemed more interested in hearing any specific complaints I might have heard against his organization. I thought he was quite a nice young man, honest and straightforward, and I'm sorry he's dead. Did he really represent the Brotherhood? He didn't seem at all the type who would get mixed up with anything shady or unsavory."

Scorchy made a noncommittal grunt by way of reply. If Miss Elvira Higgins had yet to learn MacAndrews had been a crime-busting reporter investigating the Brotherhood from inside, Scorchy did not feel it was up to him to give the secret away.

"I'm going to take these pictures back to my chief now," he said. The girl got up from the couch, eyes sparkling.

"Let me go along! I've heard so much about Prince Zarkon that I'd love to meet him. Perhaps he would give me an interview for *Borderlands*."

Scorchy scratched his red head. He thought it very unlikely that the chief would do so as Zarkon generally refused interviews, wishing to keep himself and the activities of the Omega organization out of the newspapers and the public eye as much as possible. On the other hand, Zarkon might want to question the young lady himself, so he agreed.

Using the phone in the girl's apartment, he called Zarkon at Robert Russell Ryan's estate and informed him of the discovery of MacAndrews' camera, of the pictures of the bald-headed man, and apprised him of the return of the girl and himself.

"Very well," replied Zarkon gravely. "But take every precaution while on the road—"

"Not you, too, chief!" protested the little Irishman indignantly. "I can drive just swell, it's these dang cars that just won't stay on the road."

"I was not referring to your driving but to the possibility that you might be followed by the black limousine Miss Higgins describes. Our adversaries may have observed her discovery of the camera, and if indeed the photograph you remarked upon discloses the features of their leader, they may well attempt to intercept you on the highway. Use the Squealer and take the usual precautions."

Scorchy agreed and hung up. With Elvira Higgins at his side he left the apartment and got in the car. They took the shortest and most direct route from Palma Laguna to the suburb where Russell had his estate. Once on the highway, the peppery bantamweight kept one eye on the road ahead and one eye on the rear-view mirror. In consequence his driving, never the best even under normal conditions, became excessively erratic. Muldoon was cheerfully oblivious of the fact until he happened to notice how tightly the girl was holding onto her bag and that she seemed to have stopped breathing sometime in the past few minutes.

"What's the matter?" he inquired solicitously. "You feelin' okay?"

"Oh, I'm just fine," she said, forcing a brittle laugh. "But the way you just passed between that

big moving van and the Greyhound bus reminds
me that I forgot to pay this month's premium on
my insurance policy."

It may perhaps be fairly said that the little
Irishman was just a bit defensive when it came to
remarks on his driving skills.

"Listen, lady," he began in a loud, blustering
tone. Whatever it was that Scorchy Muldoon had
it in mind to say at that moment the world will
never know, for just then they were driving down
a lonely stretch of highway bordered by thick brush
broken, here and there, by dirt roads leading off
to distant truck farms. From one such side road a
long black limousine burst suddenly, nearly creasing
Scorchy's rear fender. The girl uttered a stifled
shriek; Scorchy cursed, wrestling with the wheel.
The car slewed about, tires squealing, and came to
a sudden jolting halt as it collided with a pole.

There ensued a deafening silence.

Scorchy was slumped over the wheel, a purple
lump rising on his forehead where he had been
slammed against the dashboard. The girl, who had
braced herself instinctively against the moment of
impact, was shaken and breathless but unharmed.

The black limousine pulled around in front of
them and stopped. Four men got out and approached the rented car. They wore strange scarlet
robes with full sleeves; the hoods were pulled up to
hide their faces.

Just then the Greyhound bus and the moving
van Scorchy had overhauled a few moments earlier
came around the curve. For a quick instant, the
girl thought the two big vehicles would stop to help
them, thus probably driving the hooded men into
retreat. But they both went zooming past as if
unaware of the accident. One of the hooded men

grinned leeringly and said something to his companion, who laughed. Elvira was conscious of a sick feeling in the pit of her stomach.

Then she straightened her shoulders and set her small jaw stubbornly. Dipping into her bag, she fished out the enormous six-shooter and stuck it out of the window. It banged loudly. One of the hooded men staggered backward as if kicked by an invisible mule, clutched his shoulder, and sat down on the edge of the highway, suddenly rubber-legged. The other men crouched, cursing, so that the hood of Scorchy's car shielded them from further gunfire.

Seizing the opportunity this sudden respite afforded, Elvira reached over and took Scorchy by the arm and shook him violently.

"Mr. Muldoon! Mr. Muldoon! Are you hurt?"

Scorchy mumbled something, raised his head, and squinted around woozily. Just then one of the hooded men poked his head up over the hood of the car and snapped off a quick shot with the small, nickel-plated revolver he held clenched in one fist. The bullet glanced off the six-shooter's barrel, knocking it from Elvira's grasp. She squeaked, jumped, nursed tingling, numb fingers.

Then Scorchy came alive. His head ached abominably and he felt shaky in the knees, but awareness of their danger drove all other thoughts from his mind. He then performed a sequence of actions incomprehensible to the girl at his side: From a pocket in his coat he took out a small, flat case of heavy gray metal. From the other pocket he snatched out one of the photographs of the bullet-headed man, which he placed in the case. Palming the case, he opened the car door and rolled out, dodging a shot from one of the hooded men.

Springing to his feet, he hurled the metal case across the highway into the bushes. This action was hidden from the eyes of the hooded men because, in one lithe, continuous movement, he jumped onto the hood of the car and flung himself onto the men crouched there. He managed to kick the pistol from one man and got up, dragging a second to his feet. One balled fist traveled in a short, sizzling arc, which connected with the long, pointed chin of the man he held. The fellow's eyes rolled up and he went over backward and hit the asphalt and stayed there, out cold.

Scorchy seldom enjoyed himself as much as when he was in the middle of a good, furious fist-fight. At such moments—as he would have put it—"he got his Irish up." He generally burst into song at such times. He did so now, to the astonishment of Elvira Higgins and, quite likely, of the men he was fighting.

> O'Sullivan hit O'Murphy
> And O'Reilly hit O'Toole,
> O'Gilligan hit O'Culligan
> And he knocked him off his mule!
> A bunch o' fightin' son-of-a-guns
> Those sons o' the Irish sod,
> And divvil a one turned tail an' run,
> Which certainly wasn't odd!

Crooning this tender Hibernian lullaby, Scorchy waded in, fists flying. The two men still on their feet were taller and heavier than he, but as far as Scorchy was concerned, that only made the contest a bit more even.

He hit the first man four times in the stomach with rat-a-tat blows that flew so fast the eye could hardly follow them. Watching those blurred fists, an observer could easily have understood why an amazed sportswriter had christened the fiery little fighter with the flashing fists "Scorchy." Those balled fists fairly sizzled, they flew so fast. Then, as the man turned milk-pale and bent over, clutching his middle with both arms, Scorchy left the ground in a spectacular kung fu leap—and lovingly kicked the man full in the jaw! The red-robed crook turned a somersault, ending up in a loose heap of arms and legs against his own vehicle.

The second man sprang at Scorchy with a snarl. Sweetly giving voice to the second verse of his fighting song, Scorchy stopped him cold in his tracks with a vicious karate chop. The hard, calloused edge of Scorchy's hand caught the gangster straight across the neck. The man staggered, gagged, turned green, and sat down very suddenly, retiring from any further active participation in the conflict.

Scorchy had paid little attention to the man Elvira had shot in the shoulder. He had stayed out of things since then, and seemed thoroughly *hors de combat*. Thus Muldoon was vastly surprised when something collided with the base of his skull. Stars burst before his eyes, their brilliance excruciating. He thought he would close his eyes until the light turned itself off. Then he lay down on the sun-warmed asphalt and took a nap. Behind him, still favoring his wounded shoulder, the fourth hooded man grinned with a smirk of nasty satisfaction, hefting Elvira's six-shooter in his good hand, waiting to see if Scorchy needed a second encouragement to slumber.

None, however, was required. Scorchy was in Sleepyland. The hooded man reversed his hold on the gun and showed the cold black eye of its muzzle to the wide-eyed young lady.

"The joy ride ends right here, girlie," he snarled. "Get out of that car and help my pals into the limo. No tricks, now! I owe you somethin' for this slug in the shoulder, and it wouldn't take much for me to pay you off in hot lead. Get moving!"

There was nothing else for her to do. She helped get the three groggy, half-conscious men into the long black car, then half-carried and half-dragged Scorchy into the back seat, taking her place beside him. The man with the gun got behind the wheel. In a moment the black limousine pulled off the highway and went down a deeply rutted side road, vanishing among the trees, with Scorchy Muldoon and Elvira Higgins the helpless prisoners of the Brotherhood of Lemurian Wisdom.

Chapter 7

When Dead Men Walk

It got later in the afternoon, and still Scorchy did not come. Zarkon remained his imperturbable self, but Nick Naldini was getting restless. Although he teased the little Irishman unmercifully at times, there was a powerful bond of comradeship between the sardonic ex-magician and the little runty red-headed boxer.

"Chief, in my opinion something has happened to Muldoon and the girl," said Nick uneasily. "Perhaps they were followed by the black car, after all. They should have been here twenty minutes ago!"

Zarkon nodded calmly. "I think you are right, Nick. Menlo, fetch the others. Mr. Ryan, have you a fast car we can borrow?"

"Certainly, Prince Zarkon," said the wealthy publisher. Lifting a phone, he instructed his driver to bring a big red sportscar around to the front. Zarkon and his lieutenants unlimbered some peculiar bits of apparatus from one of their equipment cases and followed Ryan to the gravel-strewn driveway, climbing in the car. Harrigan and Naldini took the front seat, with Menlo Parker and Doc Jenkins and Zarkon himself in the rear.

71

"Mind if I join you?" asked the millionaire. "In case your friend has been captured, my presence might come in handy." Zarkon nodded briefly, busy with the mechanism on his knee. Ryan got in the front seat and closed the door. Gravel crunching, Harrigan took a steep curve and drove to the highway leading in to Palma Laguna.

Menlo Parker, holding a small instrument to his ear, snapped his fingers. "Highway accident," he chirped brightly. "Car banged into a pole a few miles on. Police radio call says the driver of a Greyhound bus saw four men in red robes get out of the long black car and converge on the wreck. Says they were probably going to the assistance of the driver of the wrecked car. No bodies reported."

Zarkon said nothing, studying the instrument on his lap. Nor did the other men make any response, except that Ace Harrigan stepped up the speed and Nick Naldini tugged furiously on the waxed ends of his Mephistophelian mustache. Ryan gathered that the instrument Parker held was a radio receiver; if so, it was of an advanced design, since it was no larger than a folder of matches.

In another few minutes they reached the scene of the accident. Four highway patrol cruisers were pulled up, blocking oncoming traffic from the far lane. When he saw and recognized the wrecked car as the one he had himself rented that very morning, Nick Naldini cursed under his breath in the sort of Italian seldom heard outside the gutters of Naples.

Zarkon suggested they pull up before the double-parked cruisers. Ace Harrigan leaned out and showed his credentials to the highway patrolman who came over to wave them on. Ryan could not make out what the aviator said to the patrolman,

but he recognized the look of awe that came over
the man's face when he realized who was in the
back seat. Zarkon got out, nodding in response to
the snappy salute the patrolman threw, and strolled
over to look at the car. The patrolman followed
him.

"Signs of a gun battle here and here, sir. Blood
on the pavement over here. No bodies, though, and
the second car seems to have driven away."

Zarkon asked if any blood had been found on
the interior of the wrecked car. The patrolman
shook his head and an expression of relief simultaneously passed over the faces of Nick Naldini,
Doc Jenkins, Menlo Parker, and Ace Harrigan.
Scorchy had probably been taken alive, in that case.
There would have been no reason for his attackers
to have carried off a corpse.

Menlo Parker fiddled with a small electronic device. A red indicator light blinked, arrow-like,
pointing across the road.

"The stool-pigeon is over there in the bushes,"
the skinny scientist confided to Ace Harrigan. The
aviator opened the car door and got out.

"I'll go get it while the chief is busy," he said.
Menlo handed him the small instrument and Harrigan went across the highway and fished through
the bushes until he found the small gray case
Scorchy Muldoon had thrown away.

Ryan had observed all this, and his curiosity
must have developed into an uncontrollable itch,
for he leaned over and diffidently asked Nick Naldini what the frail little physicist had meant by
"the stool-pigeon."

The ex-vaudevillian smiled genially. He loved an
audience and delighted in expounding on subjects
wherein he was an expert. At times like these, or

when engaging attractive young women in casual conversation, the lanky, long-legged magician waxed eloquent in a histrionic manner that exposed his secret lifelong ambition, which was to have trod the boards as a Shakespearian actor.

"Tush, my good sir, your inquiry need afford you no embarrassment," he drawled in his hoarse, whiskey voice. " 'Tis remarkably simple, after all. Each of our number is continuously exposed to the risk of capture by the foe, and, more oft than not, we possess about our person a choice and valuable item of evidence. To prevent such from falling into the crime-soiled hands of evildoers, 'tis our amusing custom to secrete amongst our garments small containers of a curious metallic composition, fabricated from an alloy of uranium. My colleague, Parker, has just tracked down one such small container, tossed over yonder broad highway by the unfortunate Muldoon—"

"Uranium alloy?" murmured the publisher nervously. "But—isn't that stuff dangerous? I mean, the radiation hazard—"

"Nonsense, my good sir!" rasped the ex-magician. "The alloy exudes a degree of radioactivity of no more harmful potency than the pinch of radium commonly found on a wristwatch with a luminous dial. The radioactivity can, however, be detected to a nicety by our instruments, and its location we are able to pinpoint, yes, even from a moving airplane."

Uranium in metal form and long-distance Geiger counters were new to the experience of Robert Russell Ryan, but he somehow sensed it would do him no good to ask questions about these surprising inventions. In this, he was quite correct. The secret of these and the other technologically advanced instruments the Omega men regularly employed were part of the secret origin of Zarkon himself. And that secret was carefully concealed from the world.

Zarkon knelt to study tire marks on the highway. He straightened after a moment, said goodbye to the patrolmen, and rejoined his men in the sports-car.

"Scorchy and Miss Higgins were carried off in a large foreign car, probably an expensive, imported Supra limousine," he said. "Are you picking up the Squealer, Menlo?"

The scientist nodded. "Over that way," he snapped, "moving slow."

"Down that dirt road, probably," said Ace Harrigan. He clashed the gears. The sportscar turned into the side road and began bouncing along over the ruts. "No wonder they're moving slow!" grunted Harrigan. Nick Naldini turned to the newspaper publisher.

"The Squealer is a miniaturized radio device we all wear," he explained. "It issues a carrier wave when turned on; Menlo is monitoring it now on his portable. That way we can follow the car carrying Scorchy and the girl to wherever they are going."

Ryan said nothing, but he was beginning to feel impressed by the smooth professionalism of these men and the way they swung into action.

When Scorchy awoke, he was stretched out against damp concrete with his wrists tied behind him. His skull felt like an egg shell that had come out second-best in an argument with a steamroller. First that goose egg on his forehead from the wreck of the car, then the clout from the barrel of the six-shooter against the back of his head. He was distinctly unhappy, and when he moved at all it was without alacrity, as if too swift a motion would cause his head to fall apart.

Squinting around, he saw Elvira Higgins some distance away, sitting up against a stone wall with her hands behind her, probably tied, as were his own. They seemed to be in some sort of a cellar. At least, the room was dark and damp and smelled musty and had a concrete floor and stone walls. No one else seemed to be in the vicinity. He decided to sit up, and did so gingerly and in stages.

He still wore his jacket, he noticed. With numb fingers he counted the buttons on his cuff to make sure he still wore the one they called the Squealer because of the superminiaturized radio it concealed. It was still there, all right.

The pockets of his jacket were turned inside out. That meant he had been searched and the photographs from MacAndrews' camera had been taken. He sent the frightened girl a grin that was meant to be cheerful and encouraging, but that ended up more like a grimace of pain because of the discomfort it cost him to flex his cheek-muscles. He was about to say something to her when one of the hooded men came clumping down the cellar stairs to show him the business end of a revolver. It was the one he had belted four times in the belly, then kicked in the jaw. The fellow did not look particularly friendly. Scorchy decided not to antagonize him with chit-chat.

With the tips of his fingers, he explored his bonds. As far as he could tell, his hands had been tied quite skillfully. For the first time in his life the bantamweight boxer wished he were Nick Naldini. The lanky escape artist could have squirmed out of these ropes quicker than you could say "Harry Houdini."

Another hooded man came down the stairs. This one had his arm in a sling, the sling hastily improvised from cloth torn from the lining of his robes. His long horse-face looked greenish, and his mouth was twisted as if from pain. The sharp medicinal stench of raw whiskey hung around him like a cloud.

"Feeling any better, Leo?" asked the one holding the gun on Scorchy. The second man gave him a contemptuous look.

"How would you feel with a slug from that cannon through you?" he snarled. Then, turning to Elvira Higgins, the injured man said: "Sister, they oughta pass a law against horse pistols like that one. Was your grandpappy Buffalo Bill?"

"Did you get the boss on the set upstairs?" asked the first man. The man with the injured shoulder nodded, then winced at the pain his shoulder caused him when he nodded.

"We got to get rid of these two meddlers real quick an' get back to our stations," he grunted. "The cops are goin' over the wreck with a fine-toothed comb, and may start checkin' out the dirt roads for tire tracks."

"Shucks, Leo, they won't find none!" the guard protested. "Ain't had no rain in these parts for weeks, and what with all the ruts in that road, it would take more than a bunch of dumb cops to trail the car here!"

"They got more than cops," said the injured man with a venomous glance at Scorchy Muldoon. "The Mick over there who kicked you silly is one of Prince Zarkon's men!"

The guard sucked in his breath with a loud hiss. There was a ringing, throbbing silence. Then he said, unsteadily, "What're we gonna do?"

The second man nodded at the gun the first man held, then nodded over at the two captives.

"Kill 'em," he said flatly. "And dump 'em somewhere. Do it now, Coker. We gotta make tracks outa here."

The second man said nothing, but gulped. Then he opened and closed the chamber of his revolver, clicked the safety off, and came over to level the pistol at Scorchy Muldoon's brow.

Fire blazed and thunder cracked resoundingly in the damp, dark, echoing cellar.

The red sportscar jolted and bounced along over the dirt road that wove in and out between heavy walls of slash pine and scrub oak.

"Did Scorchy use the stool-pigeon?" inquired Prince Zarkon after they had been bumping along for five minutes or so.

"Oh, yeah, chief, sorry, it slipped my mind," said Ace Harrigan. "Nick, dig the thing out of my pocket, will you? This road's so bad I don't dare let go of the wheel."

The magician extracted the flat metal case from the pocket of the aviator's jacket and handed it back to the Lord of the Unknown, who sat in the back seat. Zarkon snapped open the little metal case and extracted therefrom a single photograph.

"One of the pictures from MacAndrews' camera!" said Doc Jenkins in his heavy, dull voice. "Scorchy said the girl found the reporter's camera and developed the roll of film. Why just one picture, I wonder?"

Zarkon said nothing, studying the glossy enlargement. From one of the many pockets in the lining of his gray suede jacket he extracted a powerful lens and a small pocket flashlight.

Snapping on the light, he pored over every detail of the picture, examining it under the lens. His immobile features seldom displayed any emotion, but they did so now. Shock, disbelief, and amazement were visible in his face. Without comment he passed the photo to Doc Jenkins.

The huge man looked it over narrowly, then ran one ham-sized hand through his sparse, sandy hair, his dull, watery eyes glistening with astonishment.

"But he's—" he began.

Zarkon nodded grimly.

"Yes, I know. I just wanted it confirmed through your memory for faces," he said.

The man with the camera eyes wagged his massive head in stunned disbelief. "No doubt about it, chief; I'd stake my reputation on it!"

Zarkon said nothing, looking ahead stonily.

The bald, bullet-headed man in the picture was the leader of the Brotherhood, the man called Lucifer whom MacAndrews had photographed the previous morning at the meeting on the mountain. Zarkon recognized him instantly, for they had battled once before. That was not what had caused shock and disbelief and amazement, though. Those had been natural reactions.

Because the man in the picture had died five years before.

Chapter 8

The Fight in the Shack

The red sportscar bumped and jounced over the rutted dirt track that wound a narrow path between thick walls of pine and oak. Menlo Parker bent over the location finder, sharp eyes intent on the indicator.

"We're getting near him now," he said in his peevish tone. "The Squealer works just fine, chief; even after that last stage of miniaturization, the signal is sharp and definite."

The road angled about sharply. Suddenly a clearing opened in the brush, revealing a broken-down farmhouse and a stretch of cleared field. Broken windows gawped, loose screens dangled crazily askew, and the housepaint had long since worn away so that the boards were silvery from exposure to wind and rain.

"That house, maybe," suggested Ace Harrigan.

"Maybe," Zarkon agreed. "Menlo, what do you think?"

The shriveled little scientist nodded. "He's there, all right. There, or within a fifty-yard radius of the shack. Can't be more definite than that."

"Good enough," said Zarkon. "Ace, pull up

81

across the road. Condition 'A,' gentlemen. Let's go!"

The Omega men drew from beneath their coats curiously light, flat pistols seemingly made of some dull plastic. Checking them, they got out of the car, spread out in a wide half circle, and began closing in on the rundown shack. Robert Russell Ryan brought up the rear, keeping directly behind Zarkon. The big man in gun-metal gray moved as silently and swiftly as a drifting shadow, the newspaperman noticed. Like a substanceless wraith, he glided across the dirt road. His sharp, wary black eyes were everywhere, probing every shadow, every bush, catching the slightest rustle in the underbrush. Alone of them all, he was unarmed. Or was he? His sensitive, long-fingered hands, held half open, were extended and spread before him. It was almost as if they gripped weapons invisible to human eyes.

The faintest chill moved up the millionaire publisher's spine; there was something uncanny, even unhuman, about this tall, superb man with the quiet voice and strangely emotionless manner.

"Careless of them not to post a lookout," drawled Nick Naldini.

"It is," nodded Ace Harrigan. "Wonder where they hid the car?"

"Maybe around back," said Nick. But he never completed his sentence. For just then a muffled explosion went *thump!* and an unearthly blue-white brilliance stabbed from behind dust-scummed basement windows. From within came noice and plenty of it. Men yelled, bumped, fell in a clatter. Wood splintered, furniture or something went crashing over. A girl shrieked.

"In. Quickly!" snapped Zarkon.

Doc Jenkins was the first to jump upon the sagging porch. He reared back and kicked the frame of the door with the flat of his foot. Those huge feet must have packed a wallop commensurate to their size and weight, for the lock cracked with a sharp sound of breaking metal and the door broke inward, half torn off its hinges. The Omega men shouldered through it into a musty-smelling room. Sunlight filtered through broken windows on mildewed, threadbare carpet, odds and ends of furniture, a cast-iron stove. No one was in the room, but even as they entered, three men came charging up the cellar stairs and burst into the living room; stopping dead at the sight of strangers, they lifted their guns.

But Zarkon was among them, drifting like a wisp of mist, his empty hands reaching. As Robert Russell Ryan watched with astonishment written on his tense features, those long-fingered hands floated out, touching men here and there with deft, unerring strokes. They were unhurried, those strokes, and looked to be as gentle as so many caresses. But everywhere Zarkon touched, fierce, unendurable pain exploded and men shrieked suddenly and unnervingly and collapsed.

His floating fingertips touched one man on the inner wrist, just above the base of the thumb: The red-robed man gasped, turned pale as cake icing, and sat down suddenly, paralyzed with pain from collarbone to fingertips. Another man felt the delicate brush of those dangerous, deadly fingers just below and behind his left ear: He sagged to the floor like a puppet whose strings have suddenly been severed by invisible knives. The third man, a little behind the rest, saw his comrades crumple to the feather-light touches of the man in gun-metal gray.

His eyes widened; he wet his lips nervously with the point of his tongue. Stepping to one side, he raised his gun to Zarkon's midsection. And as he did so, his eyes also raised to meet the gaze the Lord of the Unknown bent upon him. Those black eyes blazed with uncanny fires, urgent, commanding, compelling.

All expression drained from the man's face. He stood stiff and lifeless, like a pole stuck in the earth, his eyes glazed and empty. Doc Jenkins came up and accepted without comment the pistol the man handed him. And the newspaper publisher expelled his breath in relief and surreptitiously swabbed his brow with a pocket handkerchief. Those black, hypnotic eyes, he realized, were truly irresistible.

"How did he . . . ?" Ryan gestured helplessly at the sprawled figures.

Nick Naldini grinned. "It's called *adhti,* one of the least-known of the martial arts, practiced only in Tibet. Precise pressure of the fingertips on the nerve centers; takes incredible discipline and practice to master it. No one outside of Tibet ever did it until the chief came along."

Just then Scorchy came up the cellar steps, limping and cursing a blue streak. The lump on his forehead was purple and yellow by now, and he had a scraped jaw and blood on his shirtfront. Curiously, his right shoe was charred black and was missing most of the sole and all of the heel. Even his sock was singed and he limped, favoring the foot as if suffering from burns or blisters.

Nick Naldini sighed with relief to see that his friend was safe. Then he threw back his head and voiced a loud horse laugh. "Too much power that time, eh, boy? I knew you'd do it! Someday you'll blow your silly foot off, you crazy hothead!"

Scorchy flushed crimson. "Sure an' if me hands weren't tied ahind me back, I'd be after strangling you to death with your own waxed mustaches, you vaudeville bottomliner!" he shrilled.

Ryan looked on without comprehension. Turning to Menlo Parker, he asked what *that* was all about.

"It's Scorchy's favorite device," the skinny scientist said waspishly. "Flash-powder in a hollow heel on one of his shoes; you can trigger it with a touch in just the right place—with your other foot, if your hands are tied. Scorchy loves it so, he keeps stuffing in more powder each time he loads it up. From the appearance of his pedal extremity, ahem, it looks like he just about blew his shoe off."

"This guy was bending over me with a gun," said the Pride of the Muldoons aggrievedly. "How was the likes o' me to know there was too much blessed powder in the compartment?" Then he grinned wickedly. "The poor galoot was so surprised he instinctive-like raised both hands to cover his eyes, but forgot he had a gun in one hand. Sure 'n he all but blew his face off!"

"Is this all of them?" asked Zarkon. Scorchy counted the recumbent bodies, mentally adding in the one left behind in the basement, and nodded affirmatively.

"Car's around the back," he grunted. "Girl's downstairs still dazed in light-shock, but okay. You found the stool-pigeon an' the picture?"

"We did," said Zarkon, briefly. "Menlo, go down and help Miss Higgins upstairs; Nick, you've got a knife, cut Scorchy's bonds." Turning to Ryan, he asked if the millionaire had a telephone in his car. The publisher shook his head.

"No matter, Menlo has a radiophone in his

equipment. Who has jurisdiction out here? The state police?"

Ryan nodded. "Chief Orville Patterson is the man to speak to. I'm afraid I don't know the number."

"No matter. Doc will know it. Would you care to sit down? You look a trifle pale."

Three big state police cruisers came in response to the call, preceded by an ambulance from the Palma Laguna hospital. The ambulance was needed for the man who shot himself at the sound of Scorchy's explosion. As it turned out, the thug had been drilled cleanly through the flesh, without injury to either bone or muscle; the medics fixed him up and left in the empty ambulance.

Names of such importance as Robert Russell Ryan and Prince Zarkon of Novenia had brought out the chief of the state police for this county himself to personally investigate the incident. He was a fat, red-faced, cigar-chewing man in neat chinos and a fancy Stetson, with a loud, belligerent manner.

No sooner had Prince Zarkon showed the fat officer his credentials and the famous names they bore, than this truculence dissipated as if by magic. The celebrated signatures on Zarkon's papers drained the noisy belligerence from his voice, and he became almost fawning and obsequious, permitting Zarkon a free hand with his preliminary investigation.

Zarkon went through the garments of the four captives swiftly but missed nothing. Not one of them had a scrap of identification on him, and utterly nothing to connect him to the Brotherhood of Lemurian Wisdom, but this was only to be expected. The long black Supra had been rented four days ago from a rental agency in Copper Springs, or so the state police reported after a swift call or two. The name was probably an assumed one and the renter's identification and license forged; but all of this would be checked out later by the authorities.

The shack was a temporary base and contained nothing in the way of clues outside of a couple of cigar butts and a portable short-wave radio through which, announced Scorchy, the crooks had reported to their superior or superiors.

Zarkon nodded, turned to the officer in charge. "Chief Patterson, I'd appreciate it if you would have your people find out where this instrument came from. It looks quite new, as if recently purchased. There can't be too many stores in the vicinity of Palma Laguna that would carry a set this sophisticated. It looks to me like an Army field radio with modifications, so you might check out all local Army and Navy surplus stores. Doc, you have noted the precise dial-settings?"

The big man nodded. Zarkon shook hands with Chief Patterson, who seemed bewildered at the swift precision of Zarkon's thought processes.

"We will be going now, with this young lady," he smiled. "You will be wanting us to sign statements later, I assume? We are staying with Robert Russell Ryan, the publisher of the *Illustrated Press,* at his estate in Seagrove. Please let me know the result of your queries; I will be particularly interested in learning the identities of your four prisoners, once that has been established."

"The one with the big horse-teeth is Leo Martelli," Doc Jenkins said in his dull, offhand way. "Formerly a gunslinger for the Rocetti combine in Vegas. Wanted in Des Moines for an armed robbery, a four-year-old rap. Believe you'll find him on the FBI 'yellow' list, too."

Chief Patterson nodded dazedly.

They left shortly thereafter, crowded into Ryan's car. It was such tight quarters that they had to double up. Scorchy Muldoon noticed this and, with a joyful gleam in his eye, offered to give Elvira Higgins a seat on his lap. Nick Naldini, however, also had an eye for pretty girls and swept into the breech, twirling his waxed and pointed mustachios and flashing toothy smiles.

"Pray forgive the oafish crudities of my colleague, Muldoon, my dear young lady!" he said in his best histrionic manner, with a low bow and flourish. "And permit your servant, Nicholas Van de Vere Naldini, to afford you somewhat more comfortable accommodations in the front seat." Murmuring a suave flow of flowery compliments, the former stage magician took the bewildered young lady by the arm and was soon cozily ensconced beside her in the front seat, which left a glowering, angry Scorchy to find a place in the back.

"Outmaneuvered again, eh?" chuckled Doc Jenkins to the little Irishman. The big man always found it comical, the way the runty little Irishman and the suave, lanky vaudevillian fought over pretty girls.

"Hush up and move over, you big goon," muttered Scorchy with a glare. "And git yer elbow outa me eye, fer th' luvva Mike!"

During the length of the trip the lanky magician joked and chattered smoothly with the girl, and looked as if he found the ride agreeable. Scorchy, however, jammed between the big man with the wonder brain and skinny little Menlo Parker, suffered in glowering silence all the way back to the exclusive Seagrove suburb of Palma Laguna.

During the trip, Menlo Parker endured the crowded conditions in a frigid silence, his shriveled features stiff with disdain. It was not the fact that they were eight people crammed into one car that so annoyed the frail but brilliant scientist, but that one of them was of the feminine gender. Among the Omega men, the skinny electrical genius was notorious for his disapproval of anything that dressed in skirts and daubed itself with perfume. Still and all, even Menlo couldn't protest bringing the girl back with them; they could hardly leave the plucky young woman by the side of the highway.

In a large, well-lighted room with walls of whitewashed concrete, a bald, bullet-headed man turned frowningly away from a panel crowded with dials and indicators. Beside him stood a slim, suave Eurasian with saffron skin and shaven pate, his weak eyes concealed behind the thick lenses of powerful spectacles.

Amidst that panel with its array of instruments, a circular screen of ground glass was set. This televisor glowed with lambent luminosity. The scene depicted within showed an aerial view of the shack in the woods, with the police cruisers drawn up before it. The camera itself seemed to be in motion somehow, as if it were affixed to an airplane or, perhaps, some manner of helicopter.

Lucifer scowled thoughtfully, thumbing his lower lip. At this expression of worried concentration, the smooth-faced Eurasian elevated his brows in silent inquiry.

"Is it trouble, Master?" the Eurasian lisped in a soft voice.

"It is trouble, Ching," Lucifer affirmed grimly. "But it is a development that has been anticipated. The leader of those men was Prince Zarkon of Novenia, an old adversary, of whose arrival I have been warned. He and I have crossed swords before, and to my detriment. But this time I have been forewarned, and adequate measures have been planned to deal with him and with his confederates, the Omega men."

"What are your instructions, Master?" inquired Ching in his whispering, sibilant tones, eyes keen and wary behind thick lenses.

"A good question," mused Lucifer. "We have two alternative courses of action open to us. Had Zarkon's interruption of my affairs been unexpected, the most prudent course would perhaps have been to terminate all phases of this operation immediately and go into hiding until such time as the Prince of Novenia and his men are called away to busy themselves in another case on the far side of the globe. But forewarned is forearmed, says the trite but accurate old adage. We shall do nothing of the kind."

"What then, Lord?"

"Sucess lies in flexibility, Ching! We must assume that Zarkon now has possession of the photographs that the reporter, MacAndrews, took of the Council of Disciples and of myself. He will identify the men in those pictures."

"Is it certain the pictures have fallen into his hands, Master?"

"I strongly doubt that the men of Group 1 had sufficient time to destroy the pictures before their arrest, so swiftly did Zarkon trace them to the abandoned farm."

"What will this Prince Zarkon do?"

"Zarkon will recognize me from the picture taken surreptitiously by the traitorous Ahriman, even as I recognized him in the televisor. Knowing that this operation is one of my schemes, he will redouble his efforts to root me out. Therefore, the second alternative course of action is indicated, and that is to strike swiftly and boldly. The men of Group 1 must be silenced before they can be persuaded to speak. There is much they could tell Zarkon that he would like to hear, and it will not take him long to unlock their lips . . ."

"Perhaps. But, Master, the members of Group 1 have been immunized against the consciousness-suppressing drugs used in police interrogation; and they are hard, tough men. Is it not probable that they will resist questioning for quite some time?"

Lucifer shook his bald head. "Unfortunately, it is not possible, Ching. They must be silenced immediately, and permanently. I have a plan whereby I can bend the sequence of coming events into a channel favorable to our schemes. I believe I can lead Zarkon and his agents into a trap, silencing Group 1 and disposing of the Omega force at virtually one and the same time."

"I fear, Master, that I do not understand," Ching lisped obsequiously. "Does this Zarkon possess knowledge of a truth serum not in the pharmacopoeia? How can he persuade to speech men previously immunized against all known truth drugs?"

"Through his devilish hypnotic power," growled Lucifer. "No ordinary human being can resist for long the magnetic gaze of Zarkon, Prince of Novenia. Why, even I, Lucifer, have felt the power of those eyes . . ."

The Eurasian rubbed the tips of his fingers together gently.

"Shall I instruct Group 2 to activate? Perhaps an assassination team, striking swiftly—"

"No. We shall employ Group 2 against Zarkon. As for the members of Group 1, I believe this situation calls for the Hand of Death! There is no time to be wasted, Ching. Prepare the Hand immediately, and summon my transportation."

The mighty man with the bald brow turned imperiously and strode from the room to don more suitable garments. The Eurasian looked after him thoughtfully, then shuddered delicately and fastidiously.

The former employers of the biochemist, Ching, had been the rulers of an oriental country who had made good use of his peculiar talents in Indochina. There, he had personally been responsible for the murder of more than two hundred political captives and foreign soliders and airmen. He never thought about it.

Cold, callous, cunning was Ching.

But even his blood ran cold at the thought of the Hand of Death!

Chapter 9

Lucifer Strikes!

To the casual gaze of a tourist or camper or even a forest ranger, nothing would have seemed out of the ordinary. It was a clear, bright, sunshiny day, the sort of day for which this part of California was celebrated.

Mount Shasta loomed against the azure sky, a mighty monument to the grandeur of nature. Wild, rugged, lonely, it seemed aloof above the world and untouched by the hands of men.

A cloud appeared in the blue. It was white and fluffy, that cloud, and nothing about it was particularly odd or curious, save for the very fact that it was there. For, save for that one white, thick, woolly cloud, the sky was pure and empty and crystal clear.

The cloud drifted across the sky and gathered about the crest of the mountain. And there it seemed to linger for a brief while. But after a moment or two, the cloud parted from the peak of the mountain and floated in the direction of Palma Laguna.

It seemed to be moving just a little faster than clouds can move and not be torn apart under the impetus of the winds. Had anyone been watching at that particular moment, he might have been curious. Even suspicious. But no one was watching.

93

As the cloud approached the outskirts of Palma Laguna, it sank lower and lower toward the surface of the earth. And then a queer transformation came over it. The fluffy surface was torn by a sudden turbulence, as from some unguessable internal disruption. Then the white vapor whereof it was composed began to shred and tatter. Soon it was whipped away upon the winds, to disperse like steam.

And thus there was exposed to view the nucleus of the mystery cloud. It was an airship of peculiar design, a glimmering metallic ovoid like a tear drop, obviously some make of helicopter from its whirring vanes and tapering rear extremity.

The odd thing about the flying craft was not its design but its color. It was entirely coated with a glassy, blue-gray enamel. Something about this odd, elusive shade made it peculiarly difficult to see. The eye virtually slid off it without more than barely half registering its image.

This strange craft sank into the shelter of tall trees and vanished from view. These trees enclosed a secluded country house obviously chosen for its extreme privacy; at least, no other homes were near, and the border of tall trees virtually hid the structure from all but the most intent of watchers.

Had there been any such, he would have seen a progression of inexplicable events. First, the roof of the garage opened like a candy box to receive the sinking aircraft, and closed upon it once it had come to rest. The aircraft seemed to be powered by an engine of advanced design: It was almost completely inaudible, even in flight. Following the disappearance of the mystery ship, a man left the shelter of the garage by a small side door. He was tall and magnificently developed, with an imperious stride and a kingly posture. His head was bald and he was impeccably attired in a sober, conservative business suit of somber, muted tones.

The bullet-headed man who carried himself so regally entered the secluded house by the back door. Eleven or twelve minutes elapsed, during which a long black limousine, an expensive imported Supra identical to the one that had forced Scorchy Muldoon and Elvira Higgins off the highway about an hour and a half earlier in the day, pulled up in front of the house. Two bespectacled, soberly-dressed youngish men with briefcases sat in the car without going to the door.

The front door opened and yet another man emerged into view. He was an older man, who walked with a slow, infirm step. His magnificent brow was adorned with neatly-trimmed hair of a silvery hue. A short, immaculate Imperial clothed his strong jaw and firm-set lips, and he wore a pince-nez clamped to the bridge of his aquiline nose. There was nothing at all odd or noteworthy about his appearance: he seemed a man of substance and position, even of authority. He, too, carried a briefcase.

Only one who had chanced to observe the bald-headed man who had, a quarter of an hour earlier, entered the house by the back door might have perhaps noticed a curious thing about the old man who now left by the front. And that was that both men had worn the same suit of clothing.

The old man with silvery hair and beard approached the car, nodded curtly to the two men within, and got in himself, taking the rear seat. One of the young men handed him a briefcase. The old man opened it. It contained nothing but an expensive pair of gloves made of the finest pigskin.

The old man carefully donned the pair of gloves

and took up a slim malacca cane with a gold ball
for a tip. Then, settling himself back in a dignified
manner, he caught the eye of the man behind the
wheel whose visage he perceived in the rear-view
mirror, and nodded briefly.

The car pulled away from the house and headed
via the shortest route into Palma Laguna.

In the city of Palma Laguna, the state police
maintain a headquarters on Powell Street near the
old Victoria Theater. It is a large building of several stories, housing rooms of files and documents,
a complete laboratory of criminology, and a small
block of detention cells. As it happened, the four
men seized at the old abandoned farmhouse earlier
that afternoon were temporarily housed in those
cells while the authorities checked their finger-
prints with Washington. It was the intention of
Chief Orville Patterson, as soon as the identities
of the four crooks had been established, to take
them downtown to the municipal police headquarters and turn them over to be booked for kidnap-
ping, attempted murder, and the illegal possession
of firearms.

The arrival of Mr. Harrison J. Porteur, however,
changed all that. His long black Supra pulled up
before the state police headquarters almost before
the last man had been fingerprinted. Showing his
card to the officer on duty in the reception area,
he was ushered at once to the detention block. Mr.
Harrison J. Porteur was not only the most celebrated and successful criminal lawyer in Palma
Laguna, but he was also a former lieutenant governor of the state, with unimpeachable political
connections.

Chief Patterson swore colorfully when he learned

the identity of their distinguished visitor, who represented himself as the lawyer representing the four prisoners. Harrison J. Porteur insisted on seeing his clients instantly, so that he might advise them of their legal rights. And, in the city of Palma Laguna, or, for that matter, in all the length and breadth of the great state of California, there could scarcely be found a law-enforcement officer so suicidally foolish as to refuse something upon which Mr. Harrison J. Porteur insisted.

"Show him to the cellblock, dang it," the state police chief growled. "He can have twenty minutes, but no more. And be shore an officer is present at the time. These are desperate men, dang it all. And dang all politicians, anyway!"

Mr. Harrison J. Porteur entered the cell where the four captives were being held. He introduced himself pompously, and insisted on shaking hands all around. The four men, it was later reported to Chief Patterson, did not seem particularly surprised or even impressed that so distinguished a senior member of the state bar should have been chosen to represent them. In low, confidential terms, the famous lawyer informed them of their rights, cautioned them against replying to any questions unless he, himself, or one of his staff, was present at the time, and warned them against signing any statement or confession. Then, advising them that he would propose them for bail at the first hearing, the dignified old man left the cell, left the building, entered his car, and drove away.

Twenty minutes passed.

Suddenly the cellblock exploded in an uproar of terrified, agonized screams. Alarms rang out, police officers came pelting down the hall on the double to the block of cells. Therein the four pri-

soners writhed on the floor, their features ghastly
and pallid and bedewed with sweat, their screams
redolent of unendurable agony.

One by one they expired within seconds.

The police surgeon pronounced them dead
seven minutes later. He could give no reason for
their singular and untimely demise. They had died
of no apparent cause whatsoever.

Chief Orville Patterson did not curse upon this
occasion. His emotions were truly beyond the ability of words to describe. Upon his sunburned, perspiring brow he wore a brand new Stetson, an
expensive masculine chapeau of the kind favored
by western sheriffs on television and the silver
screen. The ten-gallon headgear had been purchased by Chief Patterson only the day before.
This was the first opportunity he had found to wear
it.

Chief Patterson was inordinately proud of this
new addition to his cranial wardrobe. He was firmly
of the opinion that it added considerably to the
dignity and impressiveness of his appearance—an
opinion, I might add, that was not in the least
shared by Mrs. Patterson.

Despite his fondness and attachment for the
spotless and expensive new Stetson, the emotions
that boiled and seethed within the breast of Chief
Patterson pleaded with a thousand eloquent tongues
for some expression beyond the vulgarly verbal.

Chief Patterson took his broad-brimmed new
Stetson from off his brow, placed the hat carefully
in the center of the floor, and then jumped up and
down upon it until the exquisite item of headwear
had been trampled into utter and complete ruin.

Then he flung himself down in a chair, mopped
his streaming brow with a bandanna no less

scarlet than was that item of his physiognomy, and commanded his assistant to get him Prince Zarkon on the phone at the suburban home of the publisher of the Los Angeles *Illustrated Press*.

When Zarkon returned the receiver to its cradle, his face, normally expressionless, was tense and grim.

"What's up, chief?" inquired Scorchy Muldoon.

"Our adversary has moved a bit quicker than I had expected," said Zarkon gravely. "I blame myself: I should have anticipated this, knowing his alacrity."

"Chief, what are you talking about?" asked Doc Jenkins, his watery blue eyes puzzled.

"The four men we captured today are already dead."

The five Omega men looked at one another blankly.

"Dead? What happened to them?" snapped Menlo Parker in his peevish manner.

Zarkon shrugged. "They seem to have been murdered by Harrison J. Porteur," he said grimly.

Doc Jenkins' mouth fell open. After some thirty seconds, he remembered to close it.

Now Robert Russell Ryan stepped forward. His fine, aristocratic features mirrored his distress and incredulousness.

"That's absolutely impossible!" he said flatly. "Why, Harrison is one of my best and oldest friends, a man of the most unquestioned integrity—"

"It's even more impossible than you might imagine," Zarkon rejoined, with just a trace of grim humor in his voice. "Especially since Harrison

J. Porteur has been in Boston attending a congress
of the American Bar Association since last Friday!"

Ryan paled and bit his lip. When he spoke, his
voice was a hoarse whisper.

"Lucifer," he said.

Zarkon nodded. "Lucifer," he repeated. "He
has beaten us to the punch, as Scorchy might say.
However, it may turn out for the best, in the end."

"How do you figure that, chief?" demanded Nick
Naldini in his lazy drawl.

"We now have four fresh corpses, each one ap-
parently slain by the same unknown method by
which Lucifer disposed of MacAndrews," the Man
of Mysteries replied. "We are too late to examine
the corpse of the unfortunate reporter, but we are
not too late to study the bodies of the four murdered gangsters. Lucifer had to get them out of the
way quickly before I had a chance to question
them at length; he knows my abilities from of old,
and he knows that I could break through any ob-
stinacy or conditioning he could devise. I intend
to perform the autopsies personally. If we can
learn the secret of the mystery deaths, we may not
only have a clue to the whereabouts of Lucifer's
secret headquarters, but also perhaps even discover
a way to prevent him from committing new murders by this unknown method. Ryan, we will take
two cars this time, for I will need certain equipment that is rather bulky. Doc, get equipment case
14, will you? And load it in the car. We leave
immediately for state police headquarters."

The Omega men went into action while Robert
Russell Ryan called his chauffeur and ordered two
cars brought around to the front.

Scorchy tugged at Nick Naldini's arm and drew

him aside as they stood under the porte-cochere waiting the arrival of their new transportation.

"Hey, Nick, does anything strike you as kind of funny about this business?" he inquired.

"Funny? Funny! The whole blasted thing is funny, if you've a taste for gallows humor, boy," said the lanky magician querulously.

"No, I mean about the chief. What he said in there. I dunno," Scorchy grumbled, scratching his fiery thatch vigorously as if to stimulate the processes of thought. "Seems to me from what the chief said that he, well *knows* this Lucifer bird!"

Nick rubbed his lean jaw reflectively, tugging on his sleek little tuft of black Mephistophelian beard.

"Seems to me you're right, boy," he drawled thoughtfully, "It *is* odd, at that. You still got those pictures we got from the four boys in the red bathrobes? Let's see 'em; what with all that's been going on, I haven't yet had a chance to . . . Great Leaping Jehosaphat!" Taking the picture and squinting at it closely, he seemed stunned by what he saw. For once the stage magician lost his lazy air of indifference. He fairly staggered back on his heels.

Almost hopping with impatience, Scorchy grabbed his friend by one bony elbow.

"What is it, me bucko? *Who* is it? What in the name of St. Paddy himself and all the saints o' Ireland is the mystery?"

Despite the vehemence of his compatriot's voice, Naldini seemed oblivious to the stream of questions. He stared down at the picture in his hand with stunned, unbelieving horror as a man might stare at a cigarette that had suddenly transformed itself into a squirming cobra. Shock and utter disbelief were written upon his long-jawed, sardonic visage.

"It isn't possible," he whispered hoarsely to himself. "It—just—isn't—possible!"

"*What isn't possible,* you skinny vaudevillian?" Scorchy Muldoon virtually screeched in the tall man's ear.

Nick eyed him solemnly. Nick's voice quavered and dropped to deep, sepulchral tones as he tapped the glossy enlargement with a long forefinger. "*This* isn't. Because it's a picture of a dead man. Jehosaphat preserve me, I identified the corpse myself!"

"I think we're ready to go," said Elvira Higgins unexpectedly from right behind Muldoon and Naldini, causing them both to jump nervously into the air.

Chapter 10

Sinestro

They began to pile into the cars, the Omega men bundling aboard their equipment. Suddenly, Menlo Parker waved his hands for attention.

"Hold on, here! Whoa!" he yelled, eyes snapping angrily.

"What is it, Menlo?" asked Zarkon patiently. The skinny scientist pointed one frail, bony hand at Miss Elvira Higgins.

"We're not taking *her* with us, are we?" he demanded peevishly, his thin lips set in an expression of disapproval. Ace, Doc, Nick, and Scorchy exchanged grins; Menlo Parker was famous among them for this cantankerous dislike of the female sex. A confirmed bachelor, the cadaverous physicist had become in recent years a devout misogynist. It was a running gag among the Omega men that Menlo Parker had developed an allergy to face-powder, perfume, and soprano voices through sheer concentration of will, like an acquired taste.

Zarkon turned to regard the young woman thoughtfully. "Perhaps it would be better if you refrained from accompanying us, miss," he said quietly. "We may be going into danger."

The girl sniffed loudly and set her small, stubborn chin.

"You're certainly not going to leave *me* behind," she said determinedly. "I've already been kidnapped once, remember. No doubt Lucifer has me down on his list of people he would happily do without. Will I be in any greater danger if I stay behind all alone, like a sitting duck, than if I go along with the six of you?"

"There's something in what you say," Zarkon was forced to admit. "But I still think you'd be safer here."

Her blue eyes widened innocently. "Safer off here in this big empty house all alone, than I would be in the middle of state police headquarters, surrounded by your Omega people? Nonsense! And besides, I don't want to miss out on the fun."

"Aw, let her come along, chief, *I'll* keep an eye on her," offered Scorchy magnanimously. Nick chuckled.

"I just bet you will! If we're lining up for the honor of protecting the young lady, let me offer my own services," he said gallantly. "The last time you had her in your care, she got run off the road, kidnapped, tied up, and almost shot. Some protection, boy!"

Scorchy balled his fists and opened his mouth to issue a rebuttal to this bit of brutal candor, but Zarkon intervened wearily.

"The young lady can come with us, if she wishes," he said. "Stop squabbling, you two! We're losing time."

Scorchy subsided; Nick grinned satanically; Menlo fumed and grumbled; but they all got in for the drive to state police headquarters. Late afternoon was upon them, stretching long shadows across the highway and painting the west with brilliant hues.

In the lead car, Scorchy and Elvira Higgins shared the back seat while Zarkon and Nick occupied the front, with Nick behind the wheel. Ace Harrigan drove the second car, with Doc and Menlo and Robert Russell Ryan as his passengers.

Scorchy was still baffled over Nick Naldini's violent reaction to the bald, bullet-head man in MacAndrews' photograph, whom the magician had seemed to recognize.

"Chief, what's all this about this bird, Lucifer? What you were sayin' back at the house gives me the notion you know the guy from somewhere; and Nick, too. Right?"

"That's correct, Scorchy," said Zarkon somberly. "His real name, or at least the name under which he was known at the occasion of our first encounter, was Sinestro."

"Sinestro," repeated Scorchy Muldoon to himself, his brow wrinkling with thought. "Sinestro . . . boy, that sure does sound familiar, but I just can't place it. When did we ever tangle with a crook by that name, chief?"

"He is not a crook exactly, but a brilliant if deranged scientist. And my first encounter with him was five years ago, which was before you joined Omega, which explains why the man is unfamiliar to you," replied the man in gunmetal gray.

Scorchy sat up, eyes sparkling. "Sinestro! Why, sure! You mean Dr. Zandor Sinestro, the famous inventor. The one who went bad and tried to blackmail the U. S. Government with a stolen H bomb!"

"That's the man," nodded Zarkon heavily.

"Wasn't he sent to prison for life, Prince Zarkon?" asked Elvira Higgins, speaking up for the first time since the ride began. The Ultimate Man nodded again.

"He was given a life sentence in the federal penitentiary, yes, but ostensibly he died in prison of a heart ailment after serving only two months of his term," said Zarkon. "I was out of the country at the time, on a mission, but my lieutenant, Mr. Naldini here, identified the body."

Nick shrugged unhappily. "I could have sworn the corpse was Sinestro's," he complained, looking unhappy. "You could have fooled me. I checked him out thoroughly . . ."

"I wouldn't blame myself, if I were you, Nick," said Zarkon grimly. "The corpse probably was that of Sinestro: but it probably wasn't a corpse."

Scorchy blinked, incredulous.

"Huh? How's that, chief? You mean . . . he worked one of those tricks like where a guy goes into catatonia or somethin' and just *looks* like he's dead? Suspended animation, or like that?"

Zarkon shrugged indifferently. "Something like that, perhaps. We have no way of really knowing just how the trick was worked right now, nor does it particularly matter. It served to free him from the penitentiary without causing a general manhunt for an escaped convict. After all, nobody is looking for a man who's dead and buried. It's only one of the mysterious factors involved in this case; when we've cracked the case itself, perhaps we will have the answers to the other riddles."

"I should have insisted they perform an autopsy on the corpse," groaned Nick Naldini in a hollow voice. "Faking dead is one thing: I'd like to see Sinestro come back after a couple of prison doctors had carved him up to take a squint at his liver!"

"One thing puzzles me even more than how Sinestro faked his death," Zarkon admitted, to change the topic of conversation. "And that is—why Mount Shasta?"

"Huh?" asked Scorchy, screwing up his face. "Whaddaya mean 'why Mount Shasta,' chief?"

"Just what I said. Zandor Sinestro chose Mount Shasta as the scene for his conferences with his confederates. But why choose such an out-of-the-way place, so difficult to get to, so open and exposed to the view of anyone who might be watching through binoculars or a telescope? The Brotherhood has branches or lodges in several California cities, doesn't it, Miss Higgins?"

"It does, four that I know of, at least," the girl replied crisply. "One in San Jose, one in Oakland, and two in Los Angeles, with one of those two being the Mother Temple."

"Precisely. When he could have met with his underlings in absolute privacy behind closed doors in one of his own lodges, why did Sinestro—or Lucifer, as he calls himself now—pick such a peculiar place as the slope of a mountain?"

"That is a funny one, chief, now that you mention it," mused Nick Naldini, thoughtfully.

Elvira Higgins sat up straight, clasping her huge purse with both hands, green eyes dancing excitedly.

"I believe I can answer that question, Prince!" the girl said animatedly. "You'd have to be in the world of the occult to know it, I guess, but for some years now that particular mountain has enjoyed a rather unsavory, if not uncanny, reputation."

"Why 'uncanny'?"

The girl spread her hands.

"A lot of odd stories have been circulating for years, and all of them have to do with Mount Shasta. Curious lights have been seen moving to and fro about the summit of the mountain at night. A lot of those sightings have been reported by the UFO investigators . . ."

"Flying saucers, you mean?" asked Scorchy Muldoon, with more than a trace of skepticism in his voice.

The girl flushed slightly. "I'm not myself an indiscriminate believer in the plethora of sightings and contact stories and tales of people meeting little green men from Mars who came popping up out of flying saucers," she said defensively, "but stories of lights moving about the mountain peak *have* been circulating. And that isn't all!"

"What else?" asked Scorchy.

"I've read reports by people who claim to have watched mystic rites on the top of Mount Shasta," the girl said firmly. "Campers and forest rangers and other reliable, unconcerned witnesses. Some claim to have seen groups of robed men conducting odd ceremonies of some kind on the mountain, which they watched through field glasses . . ."

"Any pictures?" quipped Scorchy, unable to take this sort of thing very seriously.

"Pictures?" Elvira Higgins repeated scathingly. "How many more do you want? You've got a pocketful of them right now!"

Nick Naldini grinned satanically; Scorchy Muldoon looked glum.

"You suggest, then, that Lucifer selected Mount Shasta because of its mysterious reputation among occultists?" Zarkon asked. The girl shrugged, then nodded.

"Sure! Strange things have been whispered about

the place for years—long before this mad scientist arrived on the scene. It's more than likely that he chose Mount Shasta, too, because the whole orientation of his phony mystic order is toward ancient Lemuria. That's a mythical lost continent in the Pacific Ocean, you know, supposed to have been the home of an advanced civilization back in prehistoric times. One of the theories about Mount Shasta is that it and this whole part of the country is a surviving fragment of the legendary continent, which was not drowned when the rest of the land sunk. So I guess Shasta's Lemurian connections worked in nicely when he decided to call his racket the 'Brotherhood of Lemurian Wisdom.' "

This was all news to Scorchy Muldoon, who listened closely to the girl's sober account of these marvels.

"Chief, any truth to this tale about Lemuria?" he piped up. "I mean, was there ever any such place out in the Pacific, or is it just the typical hooey?"

Zarkon smiled one of his rare smiles. "The typical hooey, I believe, Scorchy. Doc Jenkins can give you the full story, but I believe geologists are of the opinion that there could not have been a major land-mass in the central Pacific at any point during the history of the human race on this planet. The notion was an invention of Madame Blavatsky, as I recall; obviously devised in imitation of the Atlantis legend, and picked up and elaborated in considerable detail by one of her followers, Scott-Elliot, and later borrowed and completely refurbished by a certain Colonel Churchward, who called it 'Mu' instead of 'Lemuria.' "

Nick Naldini had been ruminating on another side of the case, entirely. "Say, chief," he spoke up, "you know, this doesn't sound very typical of Sines-

tro at all, this phony cult, this occult mumbo-jumbo.
The last time we tangled with this bird he was after
the direct route to world power through wealth and
influence over the government. This occult jazz just
looks like too small potatoes for an ambitious gink
like him."

"Why do you say that, Nick?"

"Oh, you know! Where's the money in this
racket? Just bilking a few hundred gullible saps of
their annual membership fees—it's a fair living, I
suppose, but it just doesn't sound big-time enough
to interest Sinestro."

"I believe that side of it was the least important,"
said the Ultimate Man. "Power over the minds of
men through their superstitions or religious beliefs
is an insidious thing. Remember your history, Nick.
Take the cult of assassins in the Middle East during
the age of the Crusades. One cunning, unscrupulous fanatic, preying upon the ignorance and
superstition of a semicivilized people, turned a
minor schismatic splinter group of the Islamic faith
into a dreaded invisible empire that dominated the
political picture in Palestine for a generation. I re-
fer to Hassan ibn Sabbah, the Old Man of the
Mountain."

His voice became muted, his expression somber.
"Power over men's minds gives you control over
their lives. Gordon Halleck said that Lucifer was
intimidating wealthy and powerful and influential
men, through terror and through the promise of
miracle cures and healing powers. Wealth and secret influence, through such people, and an underground organization of fanatic, sincere, dedicated
followers, led and captained, most likely, by veteran
criminals . . . there's hardly any limit to what Lucifer could do. Swing one of his men into the

governor's mansion or the U. S. Senate or even the White House itself, perhaps? No, it's the same Sinestro you and I fought once before. The difference is that this time he's being more subtle in making his grab for power , . ."

His features, usually immobile, grew sad, and there was a haunted look about his probing, magnetic eyes. Scorchy and Nick said nothing, leaving him to lapse into grim silence. They were among the few living men on this earth who shared the incredible secret of his origin, and they knew that it was men like Sinestro, who strive to tyranny over men by preying upon their superstitious fears, that the Lord of the Unknown had been sent here to fight and to conquer.

"There's headquarters up ahead," muttered Nick Maldini a few moments later. "I'll pull up across the street."

Chapter 11

The Death Secret

Chief Orville Patterson was mighty pleased to see the Omega men and their mysterious leader. The fat, red-faced man swabbed his perspiring brow with a bright red bandanna and ushered them into the medical lab, where the bodies were already laid out.

"I sure hope you can find somethin', Prince," he groaned. "This could just plain be the ruination of me, you know, if it gets out and the newspaper boys want to make a big thing of it! Four prisoners murdered in their cells, right under my dad-blamed nose! Worse thing that could possibly happen, and this an election year, too! With the governor steppin' down and the field chock-full of hot-shot candidates, one of 'em could grab on this as a law-an'-order, police laxity issue, and run me right out of my job! Dang it all, I couldn't get a job as third junior assistant dog-catcher, if they get ahold of this!"

While Zarkon got ready to perform the autopsy, Robert Russell Ryan tried to console the unhappy state cop. "This sorry incident is only a minor part of a vast criminal conspiracy that caught everybody napping, Chief Patterson," he murmured consolingly. "You, the city force, the DA, the feds—everybody! Nobody but an ignorant fool would hold you personally accountable for any laxity in this situation. We are pitted against a criminal mastermind, a criminal supergenius, says Prince Zarkon. My paper will take the lead in exonerating you from any conceivable charges of negligence, I assure you!"

"That's mighty comfortin' to hear, Mr. Ryan," grumbled the state cop. "Just let me get my hands on the bird behind all this, and you'll see fast action! Any idea of who he is—or how he worked this blamed trick on me?"

Zarkon had been working swiftly and unerringly, his hands as deft as those of the most skillful surgeon. In a remarkably brief time he had the answer. Cleaning his hands under the tap, he said: "The murderer used a poison known as *gessarabya*. A swift-acting poison that need only be dabbed on the bare skin to cause death."

"Never heard of it," said the police surgeon, dubiously. Zarkon smiled.

"I'm not surprised to hear it," he said. "The New Guinea savages are the only people I know who ever use it. Undiluted, it kills instantly. You can bring down a full-grown tiger in mid-leap with it."

"But these guys didn't keel over for quite a while after the phony lawyer left!" protested Chief Orville Patterson.

"Obviously, then, Lucifer employs a diluted form of *gessarabya*, or a minute, virtually microscopic amount of the poison," replied the Man of Mysteries. "You say he shook hands with his pretended clients, and that he was wearing gloves at the time?"

"That's right."

"All he did, then, was to have a small sponge moistened with the poison in an insulated pocket, say in his jacket. Just before he entered the cell he must have unobtrusively slipped his hand into his pocket and surreptitiously dampened the tips of his specially gloved fingers against the sponge. He must have timed it to a nicety, having calculated well in advance just how swiftly the application would kill a grown man."

"But what about the death of MacAndrews?" protested Robert Russell Ryan. "According to the photographs MacAndrews took just minutes before he was murdered, Lucifer had bare hands."

"He may have worn flesh-colored gloves," said Zarkon, "or he may have previously immunized himself so that he could apply the poison without harm to his own person. The pharmacopoeia contains a simple specific against the poison, developed years ago by British chemists troubled by uprising among the savages."

Chief Patterson scratched his head dubiously. "I don't quite get it," he said. "You say this reporter fellow was killed by the same dad-burned method? But he had a complete autopsy . . . in fact, Mr. Ryan here had a whole planeload of medical big domes flown in from the medical college to check the corpse out from stem to stern, you might say. How come they didn't find nothin'?"

"Yes," said the police surgeon, nodding vigorously. "The poison may be as rare as you say, sir —I really have no way of knowing without checking my library—but any foreign substance would have attracted their suspicions."

"*Gessarabya* leaves no residue in the body at all," Zarkon assured him. "One of the common enzymes in the bloodstream acts as a catalyst, breaking down the poison, rendering it harmless. It becomes a simple colloid within minutes after death, and is thereafter impossible to detect."

The surgeon rubbed the bridge of his nose with the tip of one forefinger, still dubious.

"Then may I ask, sir, how you detected it just now in the blood of these men?"

Zarkon smiled. "Not in their blood, doctor; in the brain. The poison kills by rupturing the blood vessels in the forebrain. I simply looked for extraordinary lesions in the capillary system in that part of the body. You see, I know this man, Lucifer. I know something of his ways. He has an oriental biochemist in his employ, a Eurasian named Ching who, according to CIA reports, was active in Hanoi and in Peking before defecting to team with Lucifer. The man wrote his doctoral dissertation on native New Guinea poisons."

Removing his lab smock, Zarkon turned to the police chief and said: "I'm finished here, Chief Patterson. Shall we go into your office?"

Chief Patterson fussed and fretted while Zarkon ordered coffee and sandwiches for his men, who had eaten nothing in hours and who now looked likely to go without dinner.

"What can I do," growled the state cop, "to stop this murderin' maniac? Must be *somethin'!*"

"There are several steps that should be taken at once," said Zarkon, handing containers of coffee to his men and paying the boy. "The Brotherhood of Lemurian Wisdom has four branches—or lodges, as they are called. Our consultant on occult matters, Miss Higgins here, informs me that the Brotherhood has these centers located in Oakland, San Jose, and

Los Angeles. Four of them in all, Los Angeles housing two of them, one of which is the so-called Mother Temple. And from MacAndrews' notes on the case he lists four chief lieutenants to Lucifer, who are called Nergal, Pluto, Beelzebub, and Loki, after the gods of the underworld and of evil in various of the world's mythologies. It seems very likely that each of Lucifer's four lieutenants is in charge of one of the lodges. So I suggest the police co-ordinate a raid on all four lodges in order to arrest these four men, who are the most important of Lucifer's confederates."

"Good idea," sighed the police chief, wiping his forehead and sighing gustily. "Clever devil, that Lucifer! Did you catch the joke in the names? If these four chief hoods were recruited from the underworld, he's really tipping his hand, naming them after *gods* of the underworld!"

"I noticed the pun," nodded Zarkon. "And I believe they were indeed recruited from the underworld, as you put it. One or more of them is likely to be on the FBI list, or in the 'pink book' the U. S. Attorney General maintains."

"So you think we oughta just move in and close 'em down, eh? Gotta get warrants, though. What grounds do I use?"

Zarkon suggested the four men would all probably be armed, or would have weapons in their private quarters, probably guns that were unlicensed. He added that the four lodges probably also contained illegal short-wave sending and receiving sets, according to data in MacAndrews' notes. "But don't just move in and jail the whole membership," he advised. "I feel certain that by far the bulk of the membership of the cult is made up of decent, law-abiding citizens who would be astounded to learn that they belong to a criminal conspiracy."

Chief Patterson nodded and left the room briefly to give orders to his men regarding the raid on the regional branch headquarters of the Brotherhood of Lemurian Wisdom that Zarkon had proposed.

"Chief, I thought MacAndrews said in his notes there were seven lieutenants, not four," remarked Menlo Parker shrewdly. The Master of Fate agreed.

"That is correct, Menlo. Besides the four in charge of the lodges there was MacAndrews himself, the fifth, who acted as a roving trouble-shooter to prove his commitment before being assigned a more permanent position of authority. The sixth was called Dis, and the seventh member, Shaitan; neither were present during the dawn conference at which Ahriman, or MacAndrews, received the death touch. Mr. Ryan, here, sent MacAndrews' pictures to Washington via the teleprinter in his home. Washington called back while you men were loading the car. Brother Dis seems to be a Mafia deserter who went over to Lucifer with two crack teams of hit men . . ."

"Like Leo Martelli?" asked Elvira Higgins, excitedly. "The man I shot through the shoulder when their car forced Mr. Muldoon and me off the road?"

"That is correct. Doc identified him at a glance, having committed the top-listed criminals on the FBI list to memory as part of his usual routine. Brother Dis is based in Las Vegas, having gone there just before the morning meeting on the mountaintop."

"That leaves Brother Shaitan," mused Scorchy, rubbing his jaw. "Shaitan . . . sounds like the Arab version of the devil."

"It is," said Doc Jenkins in his thick, slow voice. "The Islamic equivalent of the Adversary of Jehovah in the Jewish mythology. The name is mentioned in the Koran—"

He broke off as Chief Patterson came bustling into the room, growling and grumping. Rather incongruously, the fat, red-faced officer was carrying a slim black cane with a gold ball for its head.

"That murderin' sham lawyer skipped outa here in such a rush he left his fancy walkin' stick behind," he grumbled.

Zarkon left his chair in a blur that made all present jump nervously. Flying across the room, the Ultimate Man snatched the article from the hands of the astounded officer and, whirling lithely on his toes, flung it directly through the window into the street below Chief Patterson's fourth-floor office.

"Out of the room, everybody!" Zarkon shouted. "Lucifer would never 'forget' something; if he left it behind, there was a good reas—"

WHUMMPPH.

In midair the walking stick vanished, blinking out of existence. A huge gasball swelled in its place, churning and seething. Tendrils of dull brown vapor seeped through the broken windowpane to wreathe about the shock-frozen form of Chief Patterson's assistant, who stood nearest the window of them all.

The man gasped and tumbled to the floor a fraction of a second later. Zarkon's men, crowding toward the door, saw their chief hurtle himself at Patterson's desk, snatching up an electric fan and thumbing it into life. Holding the whirring fan directly before his face like a shield, the Man of Mysteries crossed to where the hapless patrolman lay-sprawled, caught him by one leg, and dragged him to the door, moving backward and keeping the fan before him as he retreated.

Once in the hall, Zarkon knelt and swiftly examined the limp officer.

"He'll be all right," he rapped. "A potent but harmless anesthetic gas. Probably solidified into crystalline form, painted gold, and inserted into the head of that trick cane. Lucifer timed it so the crystalline substance returned to its vapor state about the time I would have finished the autopsy."

Two officers came pelting down the stairs from the floor above, yelling inarticulately and windmilling their arms. Before they could make themselves understood, the p.a. system came on with an ear-splitting crackle.

"Attention, all personnel! Attention, all personnel! Unmarked helicopter attempting a landing on the roof of the headquarters building! Attention, all personnel! Break out riot guns and flak jackets from the wardroom on the double . . ."

"What the blazes is goin' on now?" gasped Chief Patterson bewilderedly.

"Lucifer's men, arriving to take us away," said Zarkon with a tight-lipped smile. "They think to find the occupants of the building gassed into unconsciousness. Come on, men!"

He whirled and ran up the stairs toward the roof, with the Omega men at his heels.

Chapter 12

The Battle on the Rooftop

Zarkon went up the two flights of stairs to the roof in long, easy, effortless strides, and reached the roof minutes ahead of the others, who came puffing and panting after, with the fat state cop, wheezing and blowing like a beached whale, far in the rear.

Sprinting across the flat, open space, Zarkon crouched in the shelter of an air vent whose heavy sheet metal ought to be sufficient to deflect any bullets that might come his way.

The next to reach the roof was Elvira Higgins. The plucky girl occultist, the joyous glint of battle sparkling in her eyes, clenched in one little fist the huge horse pistol that was a relic of her grandfather. She crouched low and moved across the roof to join Zarkon behind the metal shelter. Close behind her came Scorchy Muldoon and Nick Naldini. Even when under attack, as now, the scrappy pair were arguing, both vying for the honor of "protecting" the attractive red-headed girl.

"Stop shovin', you long drink o' water, or I'll be after gittin' me Irish up!" growled the peppery son of the Emerald Isle.

"You do that, boy," sneered the lanky magician venomously, "and I'll pull a rabbit out of my hat and shove him down your fat throat until you choke on him!"

"Oh, yeah? You vaudeville phony! Sure an' the loikes o' you couldn't be after pullin' anythin' out o' yer hat outside of a handful o' cooties!"

"For the love of gosh, will you two clowns lay off the jokes!" protested Ace Harrigan in a hoarse whisper from behind the skylight where he lay sprawled with the skinny, bad-tempered scientist, Menlo Parker. Growling and snapping, the two let the argument fizzle out.

"Miss Higgins, you shouldn't be here," admonished Zarkon sternly, but keeping his voice low. "This is no place for a woman; in a minute more, bullets are going to be buzzing around here like a swarm of bees."

"Don't worry about me, Prince Zarkon," the girl said firmly. "I'll send a few buzzing on my own!" And, so speaking, she showed him the six-shooter. He grinned.

"Well, even armed with a bit of field artillery of such prodigious caliber, it's unwise," he said. "Still, you're here now, and you might as well stay; but keep your head down, and keep hidden!"

"Yes, Your Highness," she said meekly. The light of hero worship gleamed in her bright green eyes. The lithe, tanned, and handsome young man beside her was something new and unique in the young lady's experience with men. Earlier in the day he had tackled with his bare hands three armed and desperate criminals, disposing of them in seconds with a touch of his fingers. She had just watched him conduct a skillful and delicate operation on a dead man's brain, identifying in just minutes a rare and subtle untraceable poison unknown in the Western world, which had defied a team of expert specialists from one of the nation's leading medical schools. Now he was about to fight off a 'copterful of desperadoes in a daring night raid on the headquarters of the state police. Was it any wonder this amazing superman kindled a worshipful admiration in her eyes!

Observing the dazed, fascinated expression on the girl's face, Scorchy scowled blackly and punched Nick Naldini in the shoulder to draw his attention to her disgusting exhibition of worship.

"Sure and I'd be after bein' grateful to ye, me bucko, if ye could explain why it is that ivver time a handsome colleen gets mixed up in a fracas o' ours, she goes ga-ga over the chief there, and divvil a glance or a thought for the loikes o' us?" he glowered, his brogue thickening his tongue.

Nick sighed, shoulders slumping. "And she was mighty nice on the eyes, that one! Ah, hell, the chief's as bad as Menlo, when it comes to girls— never looks at 'em twice. Now shut up, will you? They're about to land. And knock off that disgusting brogue; you sound like Barry Fitzgerald trying out for a part in a road company production of *Abie's Irish Rose!*"

The huge helicopter touched down on the tarpaper rooftop of the building and the 'copter's vanes slowed, their blurry disc separating into slim blades. Red-robed men swarmed out of the capacious craft, gas masks concealing their faces, carbines and automatics clutched in their hands. Because the night was dark and overcast and, thus far at any rate, moonless, the red-robed hoodlums had not spied the Omega men and the state cops as they came scuttling out of the stairwell to find hiding places about the roof. The red-robed men seemed

to have no suspicions that the gas bomb planted by
their leader had been discovered and thrown out of
a window before it could strike down and im-
mobilize the occupants of the building.

Crouched behind the skylight, Ace Harrigan
peered wonderingly at the mysterious craft. In the
dimness of night, its curiously eye-twisting color
made it almost invisible. But the teardrop curve of
the fusilage could be seen where it eclipsed the
lighted windows of the tall building beyond the
state police headquarters.

"Cripes, Menlo, look at that," marveled the aviator with awe and speculation in his tones. "Damned
if I ever saw a chopper with the lines of that one!"

Menlo Parker grunted. "Doubtless Lucifer has
introduced some design modifications of his own,"
he snapped in his bad-tempered way.

"I'll say he has," Ace whistled. "Look at those
tanks along the fusilage—those vents arranged
evenly around the whole body of the craft; wonder
what they're for?"

"*Shush,* you gibbering chatterbox, they're coming this way!" hissed Menlo. "Wait for the chief's
signal, now . . ."

The red-robed hoodlums—Lucifer's Group 2,
in all likelihood—threaded their path among chimneys and skylights and air vents, heading for the
stairwell, unaware that a dozen men shared the roof
with them, crouched in hiding. The Omega men
unlimbered their flat, curiously designed pistols and
waited tensely for the signal from Zarkon.

When it came—a low, piercing whistle, sweet as
a bird call, they simultaneously opened fire from all
sides. Red-clothed men stumbled, lurched, staggered, fell down. But curiously, there was no roaring gunfire, no smacking of steel-jacketed slugs

ripping through flesh, no eye-stinging clouds of cordite. Nothing but a chorus of sharp, short hissing sounds.

Chief Patterson blinked, cursed, and blinked again. Switching on the portable searchlight he had snatched up on his way to the roof, the portly officer bathed the clumps of fallen in a dazzling pool of white light.

There wasn't even any blood!

It was not until later that this small mystery was solved to the relief of Orville Patterson. After it was all over, Nick Naldini explained briefly that the Man of Mysteries they served had scruples about indiscriminate slayings, even of hardened criminals, and so had equipped his men with handguns of a peculiar design that was his own invention. They were powered by tanks of compressed air, and shot bullets made of hard rubber, rather than lead sheathed in tough steel. Zarkon, moreover, had trained his lieutenants in the use of these "mercy guns," as they were called.

Fired with skill, so that the hard rubber bullets struck the nape of the neck or the temple, they were as effective as ordinary bullets, but rarely took a life, knocking men unconscious. Fired in such a way as to take their man in the pit of the stomach, kneecap, or elbow joint, or Adam's apple, they incapacitated men through blinding, excruciating pain, causing lapse of consciousness but rarely death or even serious injury. It was Zarkon's opinion, evidently, that a dead man could not reveal valuable information or testify in court; neither could he be rehabilitated. There was something to be said for Zarkon's notion.

"Douse that light—" boomed Doc Jenkins, yelling across the roof to Chief Patterson. But there were still men aboard the helicopter, it quickly became evident, and one of them obligingly relieved Orville Patterson of the task. A carbine barked; glass tinkled; the fat officer squeaked, cursed, dropped the shattered lamp, and shook numb, tingling fingers. Blackness closed down on the scene as the searchlight was shattered by the well-aimed burst of rifle fire.

The droning hum of the idling vanes screeched into high pitch. The fat-bodied vessel swung about, detaching itself from the roof.

"Holy Jehosaphat, they're gettin' away!" Nick Naldini yelled angrily. Pouring a sizzling swarm of bullets into the hovering craft, the Omega men sprang from their various places of concealment and ran for the 'copter.

It was a couple of yards above them now, floating for the edge of the roof. As it happened, Menlo Parker and Ace Harrigan were nearest at that moment. As the weird craft floated over them, both men sprang into the air, catching hold of the undercarriage and pouring the concentrated fire of their mercy guns into the whirling blades.

But without visible result.

Picking up speed, the craft began to soar skyward, picking up speed.

"Menlo, Ace! Let go—you'll be carried away! *Drop!*" shouted Zarkon. Even over the whine of the vanes, the drone of the engines, and the hissing of the mercy guns, his voice could be heard with crystalline clarity, due to its perfect enunciation and startling resonance and timbre.

Ace let go, fell seventeen feet, and hit the tarpaper roof. He hit with his knees bent, to absorb the shock that could have broken his ankles had his legs been stiffly extended, rolled in a somersault, and came up dazed, jolted, and groggy, but un-hurt.

The huge chopper whirred away, climbing steeply; then it leveled off and faded away into the moonless dark.

Scorchy whooshed, letting out a long-pent breath.

"Well, what the heck, we got a jailful o' prisoners out of it, anyway," he grinned cheerfully. "*Live* ones, too, this time!" Then he sobered, grin fading. "Hey," he barked. "Where's . . . Menlo?"

"Huh?" grunted Doc Jenkins, peering around blankly. "Menlo? Why, he's—uh—"

They searched the roof swiftly. Menlo Parker was nowhere to be found.

The shriveled, peevish little scientist must still be clinging to the undercarriage of Lucifer's helicop-ter!

Chapter 13

"N-S-D-M-T"

State police headquarters was a scene of turmoil and confusion. Zarkon and the Omega men, together with a pale, perspiring Robert Russell Ryan and a tense but bright-eyed Miss Elvira Higgins, descended to Chief Patterson's office on the fourth floor of the building.

They found the police chief's assistant, whom Zarkon had earlier rescued from the gas-filled room, mostly recovered from the effects of the insidious vapor. The young patrolman was pale and weak and shaky, complaining of nausea and a splitting headache, but seemed otherwise to have all but fully recovered from the gas. Zarkon directed Ace Harrigan to help the patrolman down to the infirmary floor for medical treatment.

A few moments later, Chief Orville Patterson joined them in his office, red-faced as ever, mopping his streaming brow with a bandanna handkerchief of violent hue.

"My boys got them birds locked up all nice and comfy," the fat man said with satisfaction. "*That* oughta teach them crooks better'n to try to raid my headquarters again! Dad-blast it all, I never heard o' such nerve, tryin' to land a chopper on the roof o' police headquarters! This here Lucifer must think he's the biggest thing come along since Al Capone!"

Zarkon nodded seriously.

"Lucifer is a megalomaniac with ambitious dreams beyond the criminous scope of the ordinary gangland crime lord," he affirmed. "Unfortunately, he is a scientific genius—one of the greatest inventors since Thomas Alva Edison, and has therefore the power to fulfill those mad schemes, unless we are able to stop them."

"Well, we'll do everythin' we can to put him under lock an' key," Chief Patterson swore. The fat, red-faced man looked distinctly uncomfortable. "Lissen here, Prince, I sure am sorry about that man o' yours! Imagine, carryin' him off like that, an' from the roof of police headquarters, too! Anything we can do to help you get him back, just say the word, dang it all!"

Zarkon had been thinking about contingencies.

"That is kind of you, Chief Patterson. We will accept your offer gratefully. I imagine the highway patrol division of your force maintains a fleet of helicopters to monitor traffic?"

"We shore do!"

"And to catch vehicles breaking the laws against speeding on the state highways?"

"Yep!"

"Then your 'copters will be equipped with radar apparatus, I assume?"

"Right again," said Chief Patterson, with a shrewd light glinting in his eyes. He grinned a ferocious grin. "I git it! You think we can folly thet 'copter by radar to Lucifer's secret hideout?"

"It's worth a try," said Zarkon grimly.

"It shore is!" swore the fat officer, the joyous

glint of battle gleaming in his eye. "Golly Moses,
let me git to th' radio room! I'll have ever' chopper
in th' county on they trail before they land!"

The red-faced man bustled from the room. Zarkon turned to Doc Jenkins, who stood sheepishly,
shuffling his weight from one big foot to another,
alternately clenching and unclenching his huge
hands into fists. The man with the tape-recorder
brain was closest of them all to the waspish, short-
tempered little savant and suffered acutely from
the danger his little comrade was in.

"Doc, you unloaded the equipment cases from
the car when we arrived, didn't you?"

"Yep! Out there in the foyer, chief."

"Bring the radio set in here, will you? If Menlo
is still alive and conscious, he may use the telegraph-
key modification on the Squealer to send us a message."

Hope flared in the pale, watery eyes of the hulking man. He left the room, returning with the
portable transceiver, and set it up on one of the
desks. The location finder reported that Menlo was
traveling northwest of Palma Laguna. Zarkon dis-
patched Nick Naldini to find Chief Patterson and
deliver that clue to the direction in which Lucifer's
helicopter was flying.

"My boys got the blip spotted, Prince," reported
the fat officer over the loudspeaker system to the
Omega men. "Northwest in a straight line, gol-ding
it, and going at a pretty fair clip, too!"

There was a big state map on the wall behind
Chief Patterson's desk. Zarkon went over to it and
traced a line on the transparent plastic overlay sheet
with red crayon.

"Headin' into the mountains," said Ace Harrigan

thoughtfully. "Good place for a hideout among all those cliffs and canyons . . ."

"Doc, any message via the Squealer yet?" asked Zarkon. The huge, oafish man reluctantly admitted there was none.

Robert Russell Ryan looked puzzled. The millionaire publisher leaned over to question Scorchy Muldoon in a hoarse whisper.

"What's this 'telegraph-key modification' on the Squealer Prince Zarkon has referred to?" he asked Scorchy.

The Irishman grinned, showing Ryan the coat buttons sewn on the cuff of his sleeve. "This here is after bein' the Squealer," he explained. "S'got a buttonhole in the middle of it, see? Or what *looks* like one, anyway! Really just a miniature cutoff stud; we guys carry an ordinary sewin' needle pinned inside the lining of our cuffs, see? You poke it in the buttonhole an' it cuts off the Squealer's carrier wave for a moment; you can send a signal by Morse that way, easy as pie. We're hopin' Menlo will use it. If he does, it'll not only be after assurin' us he's still alive an' all, but he can transmit valuable information about how Lucifer's hideout is concealed or guarded—"

"*Lost 'em*, dad-rat it!" roared Chief Patterson's voice over the loudspeaker system in an anguished howl.

Zarkon snatched up the phone. "How did your people lose the blip?" he asked sharply.

"Just flickered outa the scope! Just plain vanished!"

"But how?" Zarkon's question probed keenly. "Did Lucifer's aircraft descend to a landing below the level of your traffic radar, or did it go behind a mountain?"

"Neither, dad-blame it all!" roared the officer lustily. "My boys say it was in midair, clearly visible on the radarscope, an' the next instant it just wasn't there!"

"Give me the co-ordinates of the last sightings," Zarkon said. He listened intently, then crossed to the wall map and extended his crayon line to the exact position of Lucifer's air vessel at the last moment it had been seen on the state police radar.

"Very near the northern end of the Sierra Nevadas," he mused. "But still a good mile or more from any of the mountains. Curious! Very curious—"

Scorchy Muldoon scratched his fiery thatch furiously.

"How the heck does a big fat 'copter like that one just disappear?" he complained loudly. "Even if the blamed thing blew up, radar'd be able to see the pieces scatter!"

"I cannot say," replied Zarkon thoughtfully. "Lucifer may have invented some means of making his airship radar-proof, or invisible to radar . . ."

"Argon vapor might do it," said Doc Jenkins heavily. "A sudden discharge of argon vapor, mixed with aluminum particles in suspension, would spread the radar blip out suddenly, diffusing it so broadly that the radarscope would not be able to register its presence."

"Yes, that's a thought, chief!" crowed Nick Naldini excitedly. "Remember the metal tanks and tubes, and all those funny vents around the fusilage? If they all blew out argon mixed with aluminum powder, the darn thing'd be invisible on radar . . ."

"And even to ordinary eyesight, in a way," Doc Jenkins added. "It would hide the helicopter in-

side a sort of gasball that would look just like an
ordinary white cloud floatin' along."

"I think you've hit it, Doc," said Prince Zarkon,
nodding his gray head in satisfaction. "That's just
the sort of trick Sinestro—or Lucifer, as he calls
himself these days—would come up with. Well,
we know about where the vehicle disappeared from
the radarscopes; the only thing to do now is to
comb that area in person, hoping to find the concealed entrance to Lucifer's hidden headquarters."

"It would have to be within a two-mile radius of
where it disappeared from the scopes," said Doc
positively. "The tanks we saw on the fusilage
couldn't possibly hold enough vapor, even in concentrated form, to maintain the cloud in one piece
for a greater distance."

"That narrows it down effectively," said Zarkon.
"I wish Menlo would—"

"*Wow!*" boomed Doc Jenkins at the top of his
voice, making the others jump nervously. "Good
ol' Menlo! The carrier wave just broke this second!"

Zarkon glided lithely across the room to the
radio set. The visual signal was flickering off and
on.

"Long and short!" exclaimed Robert Russell
Ryan excitedly. "Your man is using Morse, just as
you suggested he would!"

They bent their eyes to the screen where a sharp
point of green light stuttered in a swift off-and-on-
again succession of signals. None of the Omega
men needed to copy down the signals; they were
all so firmly practiced in Morse that they could
read it at a glance, or at hearing, like written or
spoken letters. Suddenly the signal ended and the
carrier wave itself was cut off; the screen went dark.

"Either somethin's blockin' the wave or Lucifer's

boys caught on and smashed the gadget," hissed Nick Naldini worriedly.

"But what did it *say?*" demanded Elvira Higgins. The pretty, red-headed girl was tense with impatience and curiosity. "What did the message say? I can't read Morse code, I'm afraid!"

"Yes, what did your man communicate? I don't know the code, myself," added Robert Russell Ryan.

Zarkon glanced at his men. "Did we all read it the same? I thought so. The message," he said, turning to the impatient girl, "read '*N-S-D-M-T.*' "

Her green eyes widened.

"*N-S-D-M-T?* But what does that mean?"

Zarkon looked uncomfortable.

"I . . . don't really know," he confessed. "But whatever it means, Menlo thought it important."

They looked at one another, baffled.

N-S-D-M-T. What secret was concealed behind that enigmatic sequence of letters? Whatever it was it was the only clue they had to the hiding place of Lucifer. And they had to solve the mystery of the code swiftly—time was running out, and Menlo Parker's life depended upon their solving it.

Chapter 14

An Hour to Live

They had not bothered to blindfold the eyes of Menlo Parker, so the skinny scientist observed the secret location of Lucifer's headquarters as the helicopter entered it. The skinny scientist was seated in the cabin of the craft, his back up against the rear partition, and from this position he was able to observe his surroundings through the wide plexiglass windows of the craft.

His wrists were tied together and his hands were bound behind his back. Luckily, he was in such a position that he could use his hands unobtrusively. Plucking the long, slender needle from the lining of his cuff, he skillfully wielded it in such a manner as to interrupt the carrier-wave broadcast by the coat button that contained a miniature radio. He continued sending the message until the air vehicle came to rest and the red-robed minions of Lucifer entered the craft to conduct him into the presence of their Master.

The heavy vaultlike door to the secret hideout was constructed of steel and concrete, and the frail physicist doubted if his signal could penetrate it. Condensing his message as much as he dared, he

137

continued sending the same signal as long as he could possibly do so unobserved.

When the red-robed thugs came into the cabin to drag him out, then and only then did he cease repeating the message. He concealed the long, steel needle in the lining of his coat sleeve once again and did nothing to resist the men as they hauled him out of the vehicle. The slim, strong steel needle might well come in handy, he thought to himself; you could never tell. Used properly, you could kill a man with the thing.

Menlo did not know the small, slender, bald man with the saffron skin, whose eyes blinked weakly behind the powerful lenses of spectacles the size of airplane goggles. But Ching, the subtle Eurasian who was Lucifer's chief aide, obviously recognized him.

"Where did you procure your passenger?" he inquired smoothly. The pilot of the helicopter frowned truculently and thrust out his chin.

"I already reported about that," the thug began in a heated voice. "They was waitin' for us on the roof, and when we landed they cut loose with guns and got most of the boys Hugo was takin' down inside. The trick with the gas didn't work, somehow, dunno why——"

"Well, you brought back one of the Omega men, anyway," Ching observed silkily. "How did you capture Dr. Parker?"

The pilot swore sulphurously.

"Dang fool jumped up and caught ahold of the landin' gear," he cursed. "We carried him halfway across Palma Laguna till I notice how sluggish the chopper is, on account of his weight. We haul him inside, tie him up, and search him, but he's clean."

Amusement flickered in the Eurasian's eyes. He gestured to a glowing screen near his hand.

"According to the metals detector, the gentleman is far from being 'clean,' as you phrase it in your colorful underworld jargon. There is an instrument concealed in his cuff button, another in his right heel, and a third in his belt buckle. See to it at once!"

The thug flushed, grumbled, but bent to the task. They tore off the button that concealed the Squealer, and removed Menlo's right shoe and his belt. At the removal of this last article, the skinny scientist's trousers sagged alarmingly.

"Hey!" protested Menlo Parker vehemently. "I'm gonna need somethin' to keep my pants up, dang it!"

Ching shrugged aloofly. "Use the gentleman's tie in place of his belt," he said.

This was done; then they cut the ropes that bound his bony ankles and permitted the peevish savant to hobble from the room, with a red-robed thug at each side of him.

Menlo peered about with alert interest as they conducted him to their Master. Walls of rugged natural stone—of igneous origin, Menlo noticed —gradually gave way to smooth blocks of masonry; neon tubing flooded the .vaults and caverns of the hideout with softly brilliant glare. They passed through chambers whose walls were covered with control panels, televisor screens, and huge turbines and power generators.

Menlo keenly eyed the glowing televisors as he was led past them. They depicted plains of thick forest growth; rocky, winding trails; and mountain ledges. From this room, obviously, Lucifer was able to keep under continuous scrutiny every avenue of approach to his secret lair. Small television cameras must be concealed about the exterior of the hideout, he assumed. The man was damnably clever, thought Menlo to himself.

But his men had missed the steel needle up his sleeve!

Either the bit of metal had been too small to show up on the screen, or Ching had thought it of no particular importance to remove so insignificant a trifle from their captive.

Menlo grinned, smirking inwardly.

Things just might work out that the little steel needle would in time prove to be a real thorn in their flesh.

They brought him into a huge stone room. The floor was tiled, and the walls were of smooth artificial masonry; but the room had originally been a natural cavernous space, Menlo knew, from the huge stone spears that hung suspended from the rough, uneven roof. Those dangling stony spear-like growths were stalactites, he knew. Moisture glistened on their tips; the slow drip of mineral-bearing waters caused them; the mineral residue of many years of slow, continuous dripping built up the great stony growths.

From a great stone chair, like a primitive throne, Lucifer observed the captive his men conducted before him.

"Dr. Sinestro, I believe?" cracked Menlo with a leering grin. The bald mastermind nodded calmly.

"Dr. Parker! Welcome to the lair of Lucifer, for by that name I prefer to be henceforth known. Zandor Sinestro, as the world knows, died in prison five years ago."

"Okay, then, Lucifer," replied Menlo with a

genial nod. He glanced around impishly. "But if this is *Lucifer's* lair, where's all the hellfire? Dang it all, don't tell me my Sunday school teachers were wrong about that point! I always heared tell the Devil lived in a, well, in a region of more-than-tropical warmth."

Lucifer eyed him cordially, and even smiled.

"It pleases you to be humorous," he observed. "Very well! I admire the faculty to jest in the very teeth of death: That degree of bravery is a factor that I admire and respect in any man. Even as I respect your enviable scientific attainments and the reputation they have won for you in the scientific community. Although your genius is significantly inferior to my own, I can use a man of your learning and brillance and technical ingenuity in my organization."

Menlo Parker blinked incredulously. Then he laughed, a nasty, bad-tempered cackle that brought a flush of anger to Lucifer's frowing visage.

"Am I dreamin', or what?" demanded the skinny little man. "Are you really offerin' me a job?"

"I have always an opening in my organization for a scientist of your caliber, Dr. Parker," Lucifer assured him solemnly. "I have read with deep interest your paper on the results of your experiments with cathode ray tubes. The theories you evolved from those data agree with my own hypotheses in that area. Your monograph on the linear acceleration of high-energy particles, as well, richly deserves praise. Think well, Parker! I can use a mind such as yours . . ."

Menlo Parker pinched his thin lips together in a sneer. His eyes grew scornful. "If you think I'm going to join up with a gang of crooks, Lucifer, you've got another think coming!"

Lucifer nodded with ponderous, calm majesty.

"Do not try my patience overlong," he suggested, with an undertone of cold menace creeping into his voice. "I would naturally expect you to remain loyal to your leader for a time, but self-interest always wins out over idealism in the end. This 'gang of crooks,' to employ your own vulgar term, will within ten years form the nucleus of an empire that will displace the present government of the United States of America, and that will in the ensuing decade come to dominate the entire globe."

Menlo Parker made a rude noise with tongue and lips.

Imperturbably, Lucifer spoke on. "The alternatives to joining my organization, Dr. Parker, are singularly unpleasant ones, let me assure you of that! The lair of Lucifer does indeed contain 'hellfire,' even as your myths suggest! That invisible fire has already brought to a terrible and agonizing end the life of the reporter, MacAndrews, and of four of my underlings who had the misfortune to permit themselves to be captured alive by Prince Zarkon. The sixth victim of the Hand of Death will be yourself, unless you decide wisely to take the vows of the Brotherhood and to become my servitor!"

Menlo Parker, playing for time, permitted his eyes to rove uneasily. Wetting his thin lips with the point of his tongue nervously, he let his figure, proudly erect, seem to wilt a little.

"I . . ." he began, hesitantly.

"Yes?" Lucifer asked encouragingly.

"I . . . I need a little time to think it over," said Menlo in a weak voice that trembled ever so slightly. "It . . . well, it ain't easy, makin' a decision like that! I been on the side o' law an' order all my life. . . . I guess I need a little time to think things out."

"Of course," said Lucifer smoothly. "But time is of the essence, my dear sir! You may have an hour to contemplate your decision—not a minute more!" Turning to one of the red-robed thugs, Lucifer commanded him to escort the captive to detention chamber No. 1.

The cell was a rough-walled cubicle, cut into solid stone. It smelled dank and musty; moisture gleamed wetly on the rock walls. They thrust the bound figure of the frail physicist inside and slammed the heavy metal door.

A rude wooden bench was pulled up against the far wall. Menlo Parker sat down upon it and leaned his head back against the damp stone.

He had an hour. At the end of that hour, he must either swear obedience and fealty to Lucifer, or die horribly beneath the Hand of Death.

We shall leave him now, alone with his thoughts.

Chapter 15

The Code Message

The Omega men and their master had come to an impasse. With one of their number a captive of the brilliant but deranged scientific mastermind, Lucifer, decoding the enigmatic message was of crucial, paramount importance. The life of Menlo Parker might very well depend on how swiftly they solved the secret of the curious code signals. That life could perhaps be measured in minutes.

"Have any of you any thoughts—any ideas at all—on what this code might mean?" asked Zarkon of his lieutenants.

They cudgeled their wits, scowling thoughtfully, but no one spoke up.

"Doc, you're about as close to Menlo as are any of us," said Zarkon to the big, sheepish-faced man with rumpled, sandy hair and pale, watery eyes and outsized hands and feet. "You know how his mind works. Any ideas, any suggestions? Even a hint of the method he used in constructing the code?"

The man with the super-memory looked distinctly unhappy.

"Gee, chief, what can I say? This don't look like any code we ever used before."

"No, it doesn't," admitted Zarkon, grimly.

"Only thing I notice about it," mumbled Doc Jenkins slowly, "is that it's all consonants, no vowels. Seems funny!"

"Yeah," muttered Scorchy Muldoon, "why just consonants, I wonder?"

"Since this is not one of our regular codes," Zarkon suggested, "Menlo must have had reason to think that we *could* solve it, that it would not baffle us for long. Therefore, whatever the secret of the code may be, it cannot be very complicated."

"That sounds reasonable," agreed Nick Naldini, his black eyes, usually lazy and sleepy, now sparkling with excitement.

"Let us see if we cannot reconstruct Menlo's mood of the moment, his situation, and the thoughts that must have been uppermost in his mind," suggested the Lord of the Unknown.

"Well, heck," said Scorchy Muldoon, "for one thing, ol' Menlo had just made a discovery he knew was important enough to send us. It must of been the secret location of Lucifer's hideout; at least, I can't think of anythin' else he could of found out, under the circumstances."

"I agree," said Zarkon. "Now, the letters might be simple map co-ordinates, arranged by a number-substitution code—"

"You mean, like 'A'—the first letter of the alphabet—stands for No. 1, and 'B' for 2, and so on?" inquired Elvira Higgins brightly.

Zarkon nodded.

Doc Jenkins closed his eyes briefly, then opened them. "If that's it, then the message reads '14-19-4-13-20,'" he announced. "The first two letters might be latitude, the second two longitude, or vice versa."

"Doesn't make sense either way," Ace Harri-

gan said after a glance at the wall map of the state.
"And, anyway, we got one extra number left over:
20. Only need four numbers to pinpoint map co-
ordinates."

"Yeah, and why would Menlo go to all the trouble of working up in his head a number-substitution
code, when he could just as easily· transmit the
numbers themselves by Morse?" Scorchy Muldoon
demanded reasonably.

"Not only that, how could Menlo pinpoint latitude and longitude that nicely, just from an aerial
view from the helicopter?" asked Nick Naldini
rhetorically. "Lucifer's men could hardly be expected to hold a map under Menlo's nose and show
him precisely where they were landing!"

Scorchy slumped in a swivel chair, gloomily.

"The whole thing beats me," he mumbled. "I
can't make any sense out of it, nowise."

Zarkon had been thinking clearly and precisely,
in his calm, unhurried way. "I think we have been
approaching this entire problem from the wrong
angle," he said. "I don't think it's a code at all.
Why leave out all the vowels, unless speed was important? I think, in the last few seconds before landing, Menlo caught a glimpse of Lucifer's hideout
and flashed us· the simplest, swiftest message possible under the circumstances. He omitted the
vowels simply for purposes of condensation, expecting that we would fill them in ourselves if he
could transmit the consonants alone."

"Chief, I think you got something there!" said
Scorchy excitedly. "Lessee now . . . 'N-S-D-M-T'
. . . izzat one word or two, d'you suppose?"

"'N-S-D,'" repeated Doc Jenkins, frowning
heavily. Then his brow cleared. *"Inside!* Take away

the first 'i' and the second 'i' and the final 'e,' and whaddaya got? '*N-S-D,*' that's what!"

"And the rest of it, '*M-T,*' " began Ace Harrigan. But Nick Naldini cut him off.

"*Mountain!*" he yelped excitedly. "Mt., the standard abbreviation for mountain!"

"Not quite," smiled Zarkon. "*Mount.* The message was obviously cut off short."

"And there's only one mountain that occurs in this whole blamed mess," said Scorchy.

"Yes," Zarkon agreed. "Mount Shasta. At every turn, we keep coming back to that particular peak. It is upon the slopes of Mount Shasta that Lucifer meets with his disciples; it was at the base of Mount Shasta that MacAndrews died; and it was also at the foot of Mount Shasta that Miss Higgins found the hidden camera—"

"And from there I was followed home to Palma Laguna by Lucifer's men in the black car!" the girl said swiftly. "I must have been watched from some point of vantage higher up the slope."

"Of course!" groaned Scorchy, slapping his brow with the flat of his hand. "Jeez, why didn't we think of it before? Why would Lucifer pick such a hard-to-get-to, outa-the-way spot for his meetin's, unless he had his hideout there?"

"And Mount Shasta is a peak at the northern-most extremity of the Sierra Nevada mountain range," added Doc Jenkins. "That's where the chopper was headin' when the state cops lost the blip on their radarscopes!"

Ace was studying the wall map behind Chief Patterson's chair.

"No doubt about it," Ace said affirmatively. "Mount Shasta is about a mile and three quarters due east of where the radar blip was positioned at last sighting, just before the state cops lost it on their 'scopes. And didn't Doc say Lucifer's boys couldn't have held their radar-scattering gas cloud together for more than two miles?"

"Mount Shasta it is, then," said Zarkon. "Let's get moving! What's the quickest way to get there, Ace?"

The aviator studied the map with keen eyes. "The interstate north, then the Belaire Parkway. Must be side roads leading from the parkway to the foot of the mountain. Be a lot quicker by helicopter, though."

"Also a lot more visible," said Zarkon. "We'll take the two cars out front, park them out of sight in the woods, and climb the mountain on foot. Scorchy, call Chief Patterson and tell him we're going. Have him follow us up with a couple of dozen state troopers about a half an hour behind us."

"Oboyoboyoboy! Action at last!" chortled the Pride of the Muldoons, grabbing the phone.

"I believe it would be wiser if you two remained here," said Zarkon to Elvira Higgins and Robert Russell Ryan. "We will certainly be going into danger, and there is every likelihood that there will be gunfire."

A determined glint shone in the green eyes of the red-headed girl.

"You're not going to leave me behind now," she said firmly. "And who's afraid of guns? Not me! With Grandpappy's six-shooter in my purse, I'll face a few thugs any day!"

Zarkon said nothing, but approval shone in his eyes.

The millionaire publisher flushed belligerently. "You're surely not going to leave me behind,

Prince Zarkon," he argued. "I've been in on every piece of this case from the beginning; I'm not going to miss out on the finish!"

"Very well, I shan't forbid you to come," said Zarkon. "But you are unarmed, and we may have to fight it out. Here, take my gun." He handed the aristocratic man one of the flat, slim pistols and showed him how to use it.

"But this is one of those mercy guns of yours," Ryan protested. "You're not going up against rifles and machine guns with a bunch of rubber bullets, surely!"

Zarkon shook his head.

"This weapon is armed with steel-jacketed slugs," he informed the newspaperman. "When we face death, we must be prepared to deal it out in return. Ready, men?"

"Ready, chief! Let's go!" they replied in an eager chorus.

Pelting downstairs, they left the state police headquarters building and piled into the two big cars. With Ace at the wheel of the lead car and Nick Naldini driving the second vehicle, they pulled away from the curb and drove through the all but deserted streets of Palma Laguna toward the interstate highway on the outskirts of the city.

The moon was well up, and most of the city slept. Hunched over her bag on the back seat of the lead car, Elvira Higgins felt possessed by a mood of heady excitement such as the young lady had seldom experienced in her life till now. She had eaten no dinner, save for the sandwiches and coffee Zarkon had ordered for them back at state police headquarters. And by now it was long past the hour at which she would have put down her nightly novel on the bedside stand, switched off the lamp, and composed herself for slumber. The surprising thing about it all was that she did not in the least feel hungry or sleepy.

"What a day this has been!" she marveled to Prince Zarkon, who sat beside her on the back seat. "I haven't had so much fun all year."

"The day is not yet over," commented the Man of Mysteries quietly. "And we have quite a bit more 'fun,' as you call it, ahead of us."

They drove on into the night, headed for the secret stronghold of one of the most dangerous criminals in America.

Chapter 16

The Death No Man Can See

As soon as he had been locked away in his cell, heard the shuffle of footsteps receding down the passage, and knew himself alone and unobserved, Menlo Parker slipped the long, steel needle out of the sleeve lining and began working on his bonds.

The skinny little scientist, by pretending to half permit himself to be persuaded to join forces with Lucifer, had won himself an hour's time. He did not intend to waste it.

When Lucifer's thugs had hauled him up into the cabin of the helicopter, they had bound his wrists rather hastily with a length of cord. Once inside Lucifer's hidden lair in the bowels of Mount Shasta, Ching, the mastermind's Eurasian lieutenant, had seen to it that these crude bonds were replaced with a pair of standard handcuffs of the finest steel. Menlo was secretly delighted at this substitution. It would have been extremely difficult for him to saw through tough cords with nothing but a needle. But picking a lock with a needle is quite another matter!

Six years before, when Nick Naldini had been recruited into the Omega organization by Prince Zarkon, the ex-stage magician had been prevailed

upon by his new comrades-in-arms to teach them
some of the tricks of his profession. Among these
were some of the methods whereby an escape artist
can free himself from ropes or chains. Naldini had
assiduously taught his new friends how to pick a
lock; the tool of choice was, of course, a burglar's
pick, but in a pinch almost any long, slender bit of
metal can serve, providing you know the simple
technique.

A length of copper wire, stiff enough to probe
with, but sufficiently flexible to shape into the con-
tour of the inner lock mechanism, would have
worked better. But Menlo Parker did not have a
piece of copper wire; all he had was a steel needle,
and that would have to do.

Sweating and cursing, concentrating intently on
what his hands were doing behind his back, the
skinny scientist probed and poked and pried. A
hundred times he gave it up in despair; a hundred
times he set his jaw in grim determination, and
doggedly set to work all over again.

Finally he was rewarded with a ringing metallic *click*. It was the sweetest sound that had ever
caressed the ears of the bad-tempered little physicist. He slumped in exhausted triumph and let relief wash through him. But soon he straightened up,
for although his hands were free at last, he was
still in deadly danger. At any moment the door to
his cell might slam open and a dozen armed thugs
could pour in to bring him before Lucifer for judg-
ment.

If Mendel Lowell Parker had been another sort
of man, he might have chosen the path of deception.
He might have decided to play for further time, to
take the oath of fealty to Lucifer, hoping later to
find a means to escape or a way to bring Lucifer's

plans crashing down in defeat. After all, to merely mouth the empty words of an oath without meaning them is a small price for freedom.

It was, however, too big a price for Menlo Parker to pay. He had sworn allegiance only once before in his life, and that was when he had entered the service of Zarkon, the man who had saved him from a terrible death through an insidious, wasting disease by a medical miracle. To this moment he had never for one moment wavered in his strict loyalty to the Man of Mysteries he had sworn to serve. To swear a similar oath to another—to the arch enemy of Zarkon himself—was impossible for such as Menlo Parker. The words would have stuck in his craw, even though the vow would have been an empty one.

Stripping off the heavy handcuffs, Menlo began working on the lock of the cell door. Fortunately for the ill-tempered little scientific wizard, it was one of those doors that can be unlocked from either side. In the tension of the moment, it did not occur to Menlo that this was very strange. One does not lock a prisoner in a cell whose door can be unlocked from within, unless the man thus imprisoned is being tested—and being watched. Menlo did not think of this.

In a few more minutes he had the door unlocked. It was not too difficult to do, for the lock was big and clumsy, when compared to the small, delicate lock on the handcuffs.

Menlo inched the door open. It creaked on rusty, unoiled hinges. He peered out, found the corridor dark, and sidled through the opening. Almost at once he was bathed in a harsh pool of light and found himself confronted by half a dozen grinning guards.

The little man uttered a shrill yelp and shrank backward, cowering. The guards came forward, not expecting much in the way of trouble. After all, the little man had thin, bony arms and wrists that looked to be so puny you could snap them in your hands, like twigs.

They found out differently, however.

The first guard stopped dead, as if he had run into an invisible brick wall. He staggered back, blind with agony, streaming blood from a broken nose. Menlo kicked the next man in the jaw, breaking it in two places. The third man found himself flying through space. He smashed against the door of the cell and slumped dazedly to the floor, ears ringing.

Menlo Parker knew as much about karate and kung fu as he knew about electrons and neutrons. One of the things he knew was that, as far as the martial arts of the Orient were concerned, one did not have to have mighty muscles in order to hold one's own against an opponent.

Two more guards came forward, growling, hefting heavy truncheons. They struck out, but the frail little man glided effortlessly from the path of their clubs and struck them with a stunning prod of stiffened fingers or a staggering blow with the chopping edge of the hand. The guards sank floorward, truncheons falling, and decided to take a little nap.

The sixth guard, however, was more wary than his cronies had been. He pulled a pistol from beneath his robes and showed the muzzle of it to the little scientist.

It was a Colt .45. Menlo came to a halt, glaring.

There isn't much that even the most recondite skills of kung fu can do against a .45, he knew.

He let himself be taken prisoner again, cursing vituperatively. It had been a good try, but it was not quite good enough. Lucifer had stationed guards just beyond the cell to wait and watch in the dark, to see if Menlo was sincere in his stated desire to meditate on the offer of employment, or was merely planning to escape.

The big, bullet-headed man looked sad, as they brought the little scientist before him and reported on his actions.

"You disappoint me, Dr. Parker," he said somberly. "I had hoped you were capable of a higher self-interest than your misguided faithfulness to Zarkon. Such blind loyalty in the face of death, however noble and admirable, is also stupid."

"Stop yammering and get it over with," said Menlo wearily. It had been a long day, and not the most successful one he could remember.

Lucifer flushed angrily, then smoothed his features to their former solemnity. "As you wish," he said heavily. "I can no longer trust your word, it seems. Which indicates that any further offers of clemency in return for your allegiance would find you equally untrustworthy. And, witnessing your skills at escaping from your bonds, and even from a locked cell, it seems I can hardly afford to keep you as my prisoner."

He stood up. "Bring him near the throne and see that he kneels to me!"

Menlo swore and kicked and squirmed, but there were too many guards. At that, he broke one man's kneecap and kicked another solidly in the groin— a blow the fellow would not soon forget. But they pounded him to his knees and held him there, panting.

Lucifer towered over the frail older man, his grim, strong face triumphant.

"Your leader and your compatriots have displayed an unwise curiosity as regards my methods of disposing with traitors," said the tall man. "It is called the Hand of Death. I am now going to satisfy your curiosity concerning it."

With his right hand, Lucifer dipped into his robes, then leaned down to touch Menlo Parker with deadly fingers. As he did so, he looked into the face of the doomed man. If he had expected to see fear written in those shriveled features, he was disappointed. The sharp eyes held disdain and contempt, the set of the small, pointed jaw was determined and challenging, but not one iota of fear could he find in the features of the Omega man.

Lucifer's face hardened with just a touch of annoyance.

He touched Menlo's wrinkled cheek. Then he stood back and took his seat again.

Menlo felt a fleeting touch of moisture, but nothing more.

His eyes were puzzled for a moment. Another moment passed. Then another. Cold anticipation gleamed in the hard eyes of Lucifer.

And Menlo—*screamed.*

From a side passage, Ching entered the great hall of the dangling stalactites. Behind the thick lenses, his eyes were bright with excitement. He hurried to the throne whereon sat his Master, staring down at the captive who kicked and struggled and gasped at his feet.

"Master, men approach the mountain," hissed the Eurasian.

Lucifer glanced up from the writhing figure, whose struggles now were feeble.

"Which televisor?" he demanded.

"No. 4—the one covering the north slope."

"Very well, I will come at once," said Lucifer gruffly. He looked down at Menlo Parker, whose frail body was now lax and utterly still.

"Drag this carrion into the storage chamber," he commanded one of the thugs. "We will dispose of it later."

He swiftly strode from the throne room with Ching at his heels. The guard shrugged, stooped, grabbed the limp body by the ankles, and dragged it out of the echoing stone chamber by another exit.

A few moments later the red-robed figure reappeared. The alarm for combat stations rang through the caverns. The red-robed man drew his hood up about his features and hurried off.

Chapter 17

Mystery Mountain

They drove off the road and followed a deeply rutted dirt path that wound crookedly between virtually solid walls of scrub pine and scrawny oak. Before them, the enormous massiveness that was Mount Shasta loomed up against the sky, blotting out the stars.

Having gotten as close to the mountain by automobile as they dared, they abandoned the cars and went forward on foot from that point on. In the pitchy blackness, the cars could easily be concealed in the thick woods that crowded closely around the base of the mountain of mystery.

Scorchy grunted, stumbled, then cursed.

"Dang this darkness, a guy can't see his hand in front of his face!" he grouched. "How come there's no moon tonight, huh? I always heard California was mighty big on moons . . ."

"Oh, will your perennial complaints ever cease, you skimpy-brained pugilist?" groaned Nick Naldini in his hoarse-voiced and theatrical manner. "Due to your dwarfish and diminutive stature, one would assume you could maintain control of your pedal extremities. After all, runt, you're a lot closer to your feet than we are to ours!"

Scorchy started to explode, but Zarkon shushed him with a short word.

"But lissen, chief," groused the feisty little boxer, "sure an' I don't have to lissen to this broken-down old rummy of a vaudeville has-been makin' jokes about me height! Faith, an' fer two cents I'd haul off an' give him me left in th' kisser so hard as 'twould make his mustache curl!"

"The time for your perpetual quarreling is *after* we have gotten inside Lucifer's stronghold, not before. He may very well have guards posted, so *will* you two be quiet?"

They subsided, but grumblingly.

By now it was nearly dawn. Just the faintest trace of wan, colorless light was dimly visible in the east. It looked as if some giant had crushed a luminous pearl beneath his thumb and then had smeared the opalescent powder against the bottom of a black velvet sky.

They reached the very foot of the mountain and paused there to get their bearings.

Elvira Higgins indicated a trail that wound up and around the curve of the mountain. "That's where I found the camera," she said. Ace Harrigan looked around, then agreed, saying the reporter's body had been found at the foot of the trail, by the map in the newspaper.

"Then it is superfluous to indicate the obvious," said Nick Naldini with a dramatic gesture. "That is, that the erstwhile disciples of the villain must have ascended the mountain by that trail for their conference with Lucifer."

"Yeah, there must be an entrance into the mountains somewhere up that way," said Ace Harrigan. "It'll be watched, I bet, even by night."

"Then, reason dictates, we should go another

way," said Nick in his fulsome manner. Scorchy groaned.

"Somebody shut Oilcan Harry up—pleeze!" he begged. "Sure, an' ivvery time he opens his big yap, I've a feelin' I'm in th' third act of *East Lynn*—"

"Listen here, you half-witted Hibernian half-pint," snarled the lanky stage magician.

"Do they go on like this all the time?" murmured Elvira Higgins bewilderedly in a low voice to Doc Jenkins.

"*All* the time," the big man grinned.

Zarkon was examining the mountain thoughtfully, paying little attention to his argumentative lieutenants.

"Another route would surely be preferable to this frequently traveled one, as Nick suggests," he said quietly. Then, turning to the oafish man with the miracle memory: "Doc, just what do you know about Mount Shasta? Its geological origins, that is, and known topography."

The big man blinked watery eyes, rumpling his sparse, sandy hair with a ham-sized hand, thoughtfully.

"Well, it's the cone of an extinct volcano, for one thing, chief," he said, his amazing brain summoning before his inward eye the pages of a geology textbook he had scanned and automatically committed to memory many years before. "Fourteen thousand feet high . . . original crater is gone long ago, crumbled away and collapsed in, but there are a couple of fumaroles—you know, openings. Sulphurous gases escape from them sometimes, so the heart of the volcano must still be semi-active, to say the least."

"If the mountain was once an active volcano,

it seems likely the peak is riddled through and through with tunnels and caves," mused Zarkon. "A perfect situation for Lucifer; just where are these fumaroles, do you remember?"

"Sure," grinned Doc Jenkins, for whom the question was a rhetorical one. That freak brain of his was physically incapable of ever forgetting anything it had once seen or heard or read. "One fumarole's just below the summit," he said in his dull, dopey voice, "the other's quite a bit farther down and around the other side of the mountain from us, on the north slope."

"Let's try the north slope, then," suggested Zarkon. "It seems less likely to be under surveillance, since this path is the more obvious route to the top. Come on, men, and try to keep it as quiet as possible!"

They began to circle around the mountain to the other side. The clear, brilliant orb of the California moon, just risen, made the scene almost as bright as day, once they were out from behind the dense shadow of the mountain itself. They clambered over mounds of broken rock and shale, Nick Naldini and Scorchy Muldoon elbowing each other out of the way in order to help Miss Elvira Higgins over the rougher spots.

They began the ascent of the mountains, with Zarkon in the lead, followed by the girl, the four Omega men, and with Robert Russell Ryan gamely puffing along in the rear.

The climb was not as difficult as it looked from the ground. For one thing, at least on this slope, Mount Shasta soared into the moonlit heavens by a series of tiers or stages that were not unlike immense steps. It was like a stairway built for giants, thought the girl occultist to herself, not without a slight tremor. She could not get out of her mind the uncanny history of this place where strange lights hovered at night, and weird cults held mystic rites, and men were slain by invisible flames.

By moonlight, the scene was one of awful and tremendous grandeur. The night was silent as the grave, the thick pine woods huddled ominously close to the base of the mountain. There was no sound, except for the gasping as they breathed; the rasp and scuffle of shoe leather against gritty rock; and the far, faint sighing of the wind. Far above their heads, the summit of the mountain frowned down upon them like the knotted brow of a scowling stone titan.

Elvira Higgins felt her heart pounding against her ribs, and began to wish she had never gotten interested in occultism.

They climbed on, pausing from time to time to rest.

When they reached it at last, they found the fumarole at some considerable distance down the slope from the peak, which meant that their climb was not as extensive as they had begun to expect. The black hole in the mountain's flank was smaller than they could have wished; steam leaked from it, stinking powerfully of rotten eggs.

Scorchy sniffed, said "Phew!," and pinched his nostrils shut with thumb and forefinger. Doc Jenkins grinned, showing huge, square teeth.

"Well, heck, I said the fumaroles were sulphurous, didn't I?" he said apologetically.

Zarkon climbed up to peer in the hole, ignoring the fumes, which made his eyes water. He clambered down again to report a cleverly-concealed steam-pipe hidden just within the lip of the craterlet.

"The opening leads farther into the mountain," he said, "and maybe provides another entrance. Let's give it a try, anyway."

One by one they scaled the blister-like protuberance and slithered into the black hole, through disturbed whiffs of reeking vapor. Snarling and jostling each other, both Scorchy and Nick assisted Elvira to the entrance. Puffing and blowing, scarlet-faced with exertion, the millionaire publisher, as usual, brought up the rear. The older man had obstinately refused to be left behind on this final phase of the adventure, insisting he would see it through to the end.

Once inside the fumarole, the Omega men found a narrow, low-roofed tunnel that slanted downward and then sharply to the right. Each man packed with his gear a small but powerful pocket flashlight, which came in handy here in the pitch-black tunnel. The floor was rough and uneven; they bumped their heads on the roof and skinned knees and elbows on the jagged protuberances of the floor. The air was very bad in here, for whiffs of stinging sulphur steam constantly blew back into the tunnel whenever the winds shifted.

Eyes watering from the fumes, nursing a skinned knee, Scorchy bumped and crawled along, whispering a colorful profusion of Hibernian curses at every new discomfort.

"Sure, an' I know now why Mrs. Muldoon's little boy was never innerestid in spelunkin'," he groaned, lapsing into his brogue, as he usually did in times of stress or peril. "If I ivver git meself out o' this black hole, divvil a man will tempt me inta another!"

"Stop griping and keep your foot out of my face," snarled Nick Naldini, who was behind the feisty little Irishman. Then he gave voice to an anguished howl. "You did that on purpose, you little pipsqueak! Wait'll I get out of here, I'll pin your ears back so far you can use 'em for a scarf around your silly neck on cold nights!"

"Will you two birds pipe down," grunted Doc Jenkins disgustedly, "the air's bad enough in here without you addin' all that hot air!"

Finally the narrow tunnel debouched into a paved stone corridor. This was the first evidence of human habitation they had seen thus far, not counting the steam-pipe at the lip of the fumarole, obviously installed to discourage amateur mountain-climbers from attempting to explore the caverns. They got down into the corridor with many a sigh and groan of relief.

Zarkon glided around the curve out of sight, as soundless as a moving shadow, to reconnoiter ahead. He returned shortly, warning them to keep their eyes open from here on in, for they were in enemy territory now. Drawing their mercy guns, the Omega men crowded on the heels of their chief.

Neon tubing was set into the upper part of the stone walls, shedding a ghastly blue light. Any light at all was better than the darkness of the tunnel they had just crawled through; at least now they could see what they were getting into.

The tunnel was deserted. They followed it to its end, where it branched into two directions. One led to storage chambers and a dormitorylike room where camp cots of the folding variety were set up, with blankets and pillows, all neatly arrayed.

Cots, bedding, and all were Army surplus gear, they noticed.

The other direction was more promising. It opened out at last onto a stone balcony that overlooked an enormous cavern, a domed chamber only partially artificial, where turbines loomed and hummed.

"Wonder how they generate their power here?" said Ace Harrigan interestedly.

Zarkon laid his finger across his lips. Just then two red-robed figures entered the huge power room from a side tunnel. Behind them came a slim, diminutive figure with saffron skin, thick glasses, and shaven pate. It was Ching.

"Shall we pop 'em off from here, chief?" suggested Scorchy, hefting his flat, plastic pistol meaningfully.

Zarkon shook his head. From the many padded pockets that lined his gun-metal gray suede jacket, he plucked a fat tube of metal.

"Gas grenade will be quieter, I think, and no less effective," he said, stepping to the balcony rail.

Suddenly a harsh voice spoke unexpectedly behind them.

"Hands up, or I'll shoot you down!" it grated.

The Omega men froze, then slowly lifted their hands and turned to see who it was had gotten the drop on them.

It was Robert Russell Ryan!

Chapter 18

The Traitor Unmasked

Scorchy Muldoon stared at the lean, aristocratic man who stood holding the gun Prince Zarkon had given him back at state police headquarters in Palma Laguna. The Irishman's eyes popped with surprise and his jaw dropped.

"Is it you was th' traitor in our midst, yourself!" he breathed, clenching his lifted hands into fists. "Faith, an' I'll pound yer fine face in fer ye, ye Judas!"

"Scorchy!" said Zarkon warningly. The red-headed boxer subsided, growling.

"Drop those guns," panted the millionaire publisher breathlessly. "And you, Prince, lay that gas grenade or whatever it is down on the floor—carefully, now, and no tricks!"

Zarkon knelt and gently deposited the metal tube on the floor.

"Now get up and step back away from it," Ryan said, waving the pistol. Zarkon silently did as he was told.

The newspaper publisher was white to the lips with fear or tension or excitement, or maybe from all three. His hair was tumbled disorderedly across his high, noble brow. His eyes gleamed wildly, like an animal's at bay, and his tight, twisted features, slick and wet with perspiration, glistened in the harsh glare of the neon lamps.

"I—I swear—I'll shoot the first man who so much as twiddles his pinky finger," he panted, his voice thick with excitement. "So don't nobody move an inch—you too, young woman!"

His bright, maniacal eyes switched back to the men he held before him with the pistol. There was a feral gleam of triumph in those alert, wary, frightened eyes, and a twisted smile on his lips. It made the handsome publisher look strangely ugly and brutish.

Zarkon was watching him thoughtfully.

"There are no bullets in that gun you're holding," he said quietly. "You didn't think I'd give you a weapon that had any ammunition in it, did you?"

Robert Russell Ryan gave a croaking sound from sneering lips. It was meant to be laughter, but sounded little like it.

"More of your tricks, eh?" he grinned nastily. "You can't fool me! I was too smart for you from the beginning, and you know it. You never suspected that I was—"

"Brother Shaitan," Zarkon completed it for him, gravely. "An apt pseudonym, since the Islamic version of the Devil is also known as 'the Deceiver.' "

"You . . . *knew?*" the newspaperman croaked, a flicker of doubt gleaming momentarily in his fixed, fanatical eyes. Then his gaze hardened. "I don't believe you!"

"I didn't know for certain, but I suspected," said Zarkon. "There were only two men who knew MacAndrews had infiltrated the Brotherhood under an assumed identity: Gordon Halleck, who gave the assignment to MacAndrews, and you. You were curiously upset that Halleck sent MacAndrews in without first consulting you, although your editor, a senior employee, a trusted man, had no particular reason to check with you first. Neither did you have sufficient reason to be quite so distraught over the fact that an outsider had gained entry into the Disciples of Lucifer. When MacAndrews was killed, it had to be because one or the other of you had given his secret away to Lucifer. It could not have been MacAndrews, because he was an old hand at this undercover work, and was too sharp to make a serious slip that could endanger his life. Nor was it likely that Lucifer figured it out: He is a brilliant man, a scientific genius, but, despite his occult claims of mystical powers, he is no mind reader. From the very beginning of this case, I thought it likely that either you or Halleck, or some third party who still has not surfaced, had betrayed him."

"You couldn't have suspected me!" panted Ryan furiously. "Why, I got you into this thing in the first place!"

"An old, familiar trick, designed to avert suspicion from yourself," said Zarkon easily. "I have seen it used many times before. It didn't work then, and it didn't work in this instance. But I kept an open mind on whether you or Halleck was Lucifer's agent. I let your actions prove your guilt."

"What actions?"

"Your unusual behavior. When a man in your position, or in Halleck's, calls in outside aid, the normal thing to do is to share with him or with them whatever information you have, and then stay out of things while he or they do their job. Halleck we saw only that once, back at your home in Sea-

grove the night we flew in. He gave me the information he possessed, then went back to Los Angeles
to do his job. That was normal behavior. But what
did you do? Insisted on joining us, on tagging
along every foot of the way. The question that
occurred to me was, quite simply, why? Why did
you dog our footsteps throughout every phase of
this case? Not, like Miss Higgins here, because you
enjoyed the excitement of the adventure, because
you quite obviously did not enjoy a minute of it. I
observed you in the moments of peril, and you
were acutely suffering from tension and fear. Your
true motive for tagging along on every excursion
could only be that you were acting as Lucifer's eyes
and ears. Such, at least, seemed the most likely
explanation."

Ryan snarled, his eyes cold and his expression
nasty. The gun he clutched as a drowning man
might clutch a straw, however, did not waver. It
still pointed directly at Prince Zarkon.

"There is only one thing about your complicity
in the plot that still puzzles me," admitted the
Ultimate Man. "And that is: *Why?* Why should
you, a respectable man with wealth, social position, power, involve yourself in a criminal conspiracy of these dimensions? What could Lucifer
possibly have offered you that your millions could
not buy without his aid?"

Passion blazed in the eyes of the newspaper publisher.

" 'Wealth'—'power'—'position'!   I   inherited
these from my father," he said viciously, his voice
thick with emotion. "Everything I have came from
him   gifts, nothing that I made or earned or won
for myself! I always despised him; even now, I
hate him."

Then something seemed to come over the sneering, sweating, white-faced millionaire. A strangely ominous, dreamy expression stole into his eyes.

"Three times I ran for governor of the state," he said in a soft voice, which trembled slightly to the intensity of his emotion. "And three times I offered my talents and my services to the people. Each time I spent a fortune on my political campaign. And each time . . . the voters refused me . . . denied me . . . *rejected* me!"

He laughed in a manner that sent shivers up the spines of those who heard the laughter. There was no humor in his laugh; it sounded like bits of broken glass being rubbed together.

"Lucifer has promised me California to rule as a province of his empire, once he has overthrown the American Government," he said softly, gloatingly. "And when I ascend my throne, the people of this state will wish they had never been born."

His voice rose suddenly into a hoarse, raw-throated shriek that rang and echoed through the cavernous room.

"Ching! *Ching!* I am holding Zarkon and the Omega men at gun-point—up here, on the balcony. Send your men—on the double!"

The little Eurasian with the thick-lensed spectacles had been busied below, overseeing some adjustments to one of the turbines. It was obvious from the way he jerked his head around and stared above him, startled, that he had heard nothing of the low-voiced, swift exchange between Zarkon and Robert Russell Ryan above the droning music of the power units.

Now he rapped out a terse command and the big, red-robed thugs who had been working on the turbine went running up the spiral iron staircase, cursing and yanking at the hem of their robes as the voluminous garments tangled their legs.

They came rushing up onto the balcony, lifting their heavy rifles in a menacing manner. Ching prudently kept himself well in the rear, so as to be out of the path of flying lead.

Ryan was still rapt, glazed eyes staring blindly at some paradisiacal vision of the future only he could see.

Then it was that Zarkon whirled into action. His transition from utter immobility into whizzing motion took them all by surprise. His lithe, gray-clad figure became a blur as he hurled himself across the platform. Like a striking panther, he pounced on the fanatic, dreamy-eyed publisher.

At the top of the stairs Ching's thugs gaped, blinking puzzledly at the superhuman speed with which the tall man moved.

Ryan yipped and squeezed off a shot. His pistol was still aimed directly at Zarkon's heart. Even the superhuman speed with which the Man of Mysteries could move could not have carried him out of the path of the flashing bullet. Indeed, he did not even attempt to evade the gunshot; instead, he sprang *toward* Ryan, hurtling himself directly into the bullet's path.

But something was odd. Something was wrong.

There was no bullet! It was even as the Lord of the Unknown had stated just a few moments ago: The pistol he had handed to Robert Russell Ryan back at the state police headquarters building in Palma Laguna was indeed empty.

Ryan shrieked, dropped his eyes to the empty gun, disbelief legible in his face. He had dismissed

Zarkon's prescient claim as an obvious bluff; now he knew better.

But it was too late to do anything about it.

"Hold it, you!" growled one of the thugs, lifting his rifle.

Zarkon pounced upon the slim, aristocratic publisher, caught him by the hip and the armpit, hoisted him with effortless ease, pivoted—and threw him at the guard!

The others were clumping up the iron stair behind the first, with Ching cautiously bringing up the rear. Ryan's flying form crashed into the first guard, who lost his footing and went whirling over backward, knocking the others off balance. They were tumbling down the stairs in a cursing, blundering tangle of arms and legs and bodies, guns falling, to clank against the concrete floor below.

With a howl, the Omega men sprang into action, jumping down the stairs to club the entangled men into unconsciousness. Zarkon did not bother with the stairs, but whipped over the railing and dropped from the balcony, landing on the floor of the great room on all fours, as lightly and elastically as the proverbial cat.

Ching had dodged back down the stairs and was trying to flee through the nearer of the stone archways that led to other, more remote parts of this warren of passages and tunnels. Zarkon overtook him with a sprint of blinding speed.

The little Eurasian, his mask of suavity shattered, squealed and whipped out a gun from some hidden pocket in his robes. But Zarkon's hand went floating out in one of those curiously weightless, seemingly casual gestures that were his own peculiar mode of hand-to-hand fighting. Gently as

a caress, his fingers touched the lump of nerve
ganglia at the hinge of Ching's jaw.

The pistol fell from strengthless fingers. Eyes
glazing, Ching sagged bonelessly to slump on the
floor.

Alarms were going off now, filling the echoing
stone room with a deafening clangor. A big glass
televisor screen, set in the farther wall, lit up with
the frowning face and glaring, ice-pale eyes of Lucifer. Obviously, some hidden watcher or concealed camera had glimpsed the turmoil in the big
room and had tripped the alarms.

Zarkon whipped about and flew for the nearest
doorway. It was a huge stone arch, vaguely Gothic
in design. Even as he flung himself across the room
toward it, a heavy steel barrier dropped clangingly
to seal it off.

Lucifer laughed!

And the Omega men were trapped.

Gas began leaking in a steady stream from hidden
vents in the wall. The vaporous streams intensified
into a high-pressure jet. The gas was doubtlessly
anesthetic in nature. The power room was huge,
but such was the vapor billowing from the hidden
vents that the room would probably be filled in
minutes.

White clouds thickened, obscuring Lucifer's vision of the stone room. He cursed, fiddling with
the controls.

Moments later the white wall of sleep gas thinned
out and the mastermind of crime regained his un-
impeded view of the huge stone chamber.

Bodies lay slumped about. Some were his own
thugs in their red robes, but others he could recognize as the bodies of the Omega men. Brother
Shaitan—he who had been known as Robert Rus-

sell Ryan, millionaire publisher of the Los Angeles *Illustrated Press*—lay sprawled amid the others. So was the girl occultist, Elvira Higgins.

Lucifer's fierce eyes probed the stone room, searching—searching!

Then his gaze found the object for which it had sought. The strong mouth curved in a gloating smile of triumph. Again, Lucifer laughed.

For the body nearest to the great archway—the archway now blocked by a heavy grille of steel bars—was clothed in the characteristic gray suede jacket and slacks always worn by Zarkon, Lord of the Unknown!

Chapter 19

Back from the Dead!

Scorchy was in a mood particularly grim and gloomy. The reasons for this were several, and obvious. For one thing, he had his hands tied behind him by stout cords. For another, he was locked in one of a row of stone cells. And for a third, Lucifer's thugs had stripped the feisty little prize-fighter down to his socks and shorts.

He cherished in his mind the memory of the cheerfully grinning gangster who had pulled off his clothes with many an off-color wisecrack. That this should have happened in the very presence of Elvira Higgins was but an added thornprick in the pride of Scorchy Muldoon. In just a few short hours, he had conceived an enormous infatuation for the pretty, red-headed girl. It made him mad to think how foolish he must have looked, plucked like a chicken right in front of her, and unable to do anything about it!

The worst thing of all, as far as Scorchy was concerned, was that Zarkon was not imprisoned with them.

Zarkon's whereabouts were not known to the Omega men. He had been downed by the gas, they knew, or guessed, for they had all seen his gray-clad body sprawled on the oil-stained concrete floor.

But that had been the last they had seen of the Ultimate Man. They had slumped into. unconsciousness a moment after, and knew nothing more until awakening in their separate cells a little while ago.

Where was Zarkon? Why was he not imprisoned with his men? Had Lucifer set him apart from the rest of them for some fiendish punishment, some malicious torment, that he must suffer alone under the gloating gaze of the deranged criminal mastermind?

They did not know; but he was not here.

This worried Scorchy, for the Pride of the Muldoons loved his chief with a fierce, undivided love that was just this side of idolatry. Scorchy could not imagine the world without Prince Zarkon in it, or his life without the man he was humbly proud to think of as his master. It was the not-knowing that rankled so bitterly. . . .

Scorchy's one and only consolation was that Nick Naldini had also suffered the discomfiture of bondage and the indignity of being stripped almost to the buff. The histrionic protests the whiskey-voiced vaudevillian had croaked while being peeled had delighted Scorchy's risibilities. If he had to be forcibly undressed, the affront to his dignity was soothed and solaced, knowing that Nick had suffered the identical ignominy.

And, whereas Scorchy, although short, had a fine, compact, well-muscled build, such as would hardly bring a pitying smile to the lips of any pretty girl, Nick Naldini was skinny as a rail and looked pretty silly in his shorts.

The red-robed gangsters had come crowding into

the big stone room just as soon as the sleep gas had dissipated and become harmless. They had carried the unconscious bodies to this row of cells, then stripped the Omega men almost to the buff, permitting them to retain their undershorts and socks only. Lucifer was wary of these men and treated them with respect, but he knew their custom of concealing a variety of small gadgets and devices unobtrusively about their person, and could not trust the Omega men to be safe and secure, even under lock and key, and tightly bound, unless they had been relieved of their garments.

So he had ordered them undressed before consigning them to individual cells. All of them had suffered the same embarrassment and disgrace at the hands of their captors, save for Elvira Higgins alone. Lucifer had spared the young woman from this discomforting experience on the grounds that, not being a member of the Omega organization, she was unlikely to be carrying infernal devices. His men had, however, been instructed to relieve her of her bag and to carefully go through the pockets of her clothing in order to remove from her person any suspicious object or device.

Lucifer's instructions had meticulously been carried out; the attractive redhead had protested vehemently and loudly, but the thugs had offered her neither insult nor indignity, and she subsided once the cell door was slammed and locked.

Only one occupant of the power room had not rejoined them in the cell block, and that was the millionaire newspaper publisher, Robert Russell Ryan.

Somehow in the fall down the iron stairs, the traitor whom the Omega men had permitted to accompany them throughout this entire adventure had hit his head on a steel rail. He had died instantly from a concussion of the brain.

So abruptly ended the life of a man born to wealth, power, influence, and social position, whose overweening political ambitions made him dissatisfied with anything except high office, and who had turned to a secret career of crime in order to fulfill his unholy lust for power. It was a sad, almost a tragic, end for one born to a life of ease and luxury, with advantages denied the many and enjoyed only by the few.

But few traitors live to enjoy the fruits of their betrayals, and such was the case with Robert Russell Ryan.

Scorchy groused and cussed and grumbled for a long time after the red-robed thugs had thrown him inside the cell and locked the door. Then he had squirmed into a more comfortable position and began to work on his bonds. There wasn't much he could have done to free himself from the cell even if he had managed to get his wrists untied, since he had been relieved of all his gadgets. But the tough little Hibernian would have felt a lot better, down deep inside, with his hands free.

Unfortunately, perhaps owing to their former experience with Menlo Parker, the thugs had knotted Scorchy's bonds with considerable care and ingenuity. They had not used handcuffs this time. The reason for this was simple: To those who know the tricks of the escape artist, it is always easier to get out of handcuffs than it is to free yourself from ropes.

The lock on a pair of handcuffs can always be picked. It is not so difficult to escape from them as the man in the street may think. If it were, professional escape artists would avoid using handcuffs on the stage, whereas in fact they virtually delight in them.

But to free yourself from well-tied ropes is incomparably tougher. There's only one way to get your hands free from ropes, and that is to cut them. Without a knife blade or some sharp instrument, you're stuck.

So it was with Scorchy Muldoon. And to make matters worse, the thugs had not even used ordinary ropes, but nylon cords, which were difficult even to cut through.

After a while, his wrists chafed raw and his fingers numb with weariness, Scorchy just plain gave up. It must very nearly be day by now, he thought to himself. It had been a long and a very busy night. He was pretty worn out from all the excitement and exertion of the fight, the capture, and so on, not to mention the climbing of the mountain itself.

So he settled back as comfortably as he could, cleared all worries out of his mind, and took a nap. There was simply no reason not to snatch some sleep while he could.

Lucifer was sure to make certain he was awake when it was time for him to die.

As for Nick Naldini, the former stage magician and escape artist knew all the tricks of his trade. Even bound with a stout length of nylon cord, the scrawny magician with the Mephisto mustache could probably have Houdinied his way to freedom in less time than it would take me to describe how he did it.

But Lucifer knew all about Nick Naldini and his stage career. Each of the Omega men had been thoroughly researched by Lucifer's agents long before. And for the lanky magician, the mastermind of criminality had devised a mode of bondage that would have defied the skills of Houdini himself.

In essence, it was quite simple. An injection had rendered his hands and arms temporarily strengthless.

Nothing exotic in the way of obscure pharmaceuticals had been used to render Nick Naldini helpless. It had perhaps appealed to Lucifer's sense of humor to employ ordinary Xylocaine—the variety of local anesthesia commonly used by good dentists to deaden all sensation in an aching jaw!

Unable to use his hands at all, Nick sat back and soothed his lacerated ego by imagining the things he would like to do to Lucifer, had he the crime lord helpless and at his mercy. There were quite a few things he would like to have done to Lucifer, and the more he thought about it, the more interesting and ingenious amusements came to mind.

After a while, even this mild form of mental entertainment began to pall. And before long, Nick Naldini fell into a doze as well, for he too was worn out from the fatigue and tension of the long, exciting day.

He slept deeply—so deeply that he did not see the small, hunched, red-robed figure as it crept on furtive, silent feet past his cell.

The robed figure paused outside Nick's cell and peered inside for a moment. Then it glided on.

It moved silently and secretly, in an ominous manner.

In one hand it carried a wicked knife with a broad blade and sharp edges. It was a knife of the variety made famous by the late Colonel James

Bowie, who employed it to good advantage in the
Battle of the Alamo.

It was the sort of knife that could slit a throat
with uncanny ease.

The robed figure paused outside of the cell in
which Scorchy Muldoon snored and snoozed. Metal
clinked against metal as it drew from beneath its
robes a ring of keys and tested them, one by one,
in the lock.

Eventually, the red-robed one found the right
key. It grated in the keyhole. The lock clicked with
a metallic sound. The cell door opened and the
robed figure glided within and approached the
slumped form of Scorchy Muldoon on furtive,
stealthy feet.

Scorchy never quite knew what had awakened him.
He had been dreaming, he afterward remembered—confused dreams, full of lurking, shadowy
figures and brooding eyes glaring through the
darkness, with a chill undercurrent of tension and
menace.

But suddenly he came awake, all at once, tingling
with apprehension—to find a shadowy, faceless
form looming over him!

For a single split second, he thought he was still
dreaming. Then he saw the gleam of the big knife
in the hands of the red-robed figure and realized
icily that this was no dream.

Scorchy opened his mouth to yell. But strong,
thin fingers closed over it, clamping his jaws shut,
stifling his outcry.

Then the figure raised its other hand, the one
holding the naked blade, and pulled back the hood
that had concealed its features. And Scorchy stared

up into the face of the man who had entered his cell in so sinister a manner.

And then he had good cause to wish he could yell out.

For the face of the man bending over him belonged to a dead man!

Chapter 20

The Stone Spear

Lucifer, at that same moment in time, was savoring his ultimate triumph.

He sat like an emperor in his great thronelike stone chair, which stood in the hall of the dangling stalactites. His hands clutched the arms of the chair, as if to reassure himself by the tightness of his grip that this long-dreamed-of triumph was real and not a dream.

Through his televisor, he had watched the Omega men dragged from the power room, limply unconscious from the gas he had injected into the chamber.

Under his brooding, triumphant eyes they had been searched and stripped, one by one, the pitiful little men who had, in their ignorance and folly, dared to pit themselves against his own gigantic brain and iron will.

He feared them no more. He could have ordered them to be slain on the spot, but he wished for a more dramatic manner of death for his enemies, so that he could savor the sweetness of his victory to the full. Let them be bound securely and locked in separate cells, he had commanded. Later there would be a mass execution, to be celebrated with due formality.

And so they were taken away.

All but their leader.

As for the sprawled, unconscious figure of the man in the rumpled gray suede, Lucifer commanded that he be brought to the foot of the throne.

And then Lucifer had entered the throne room, stepping over the drugged and senseless body of his archenemy, to ascend the throne. The act pleased him in its symbolism.

He looked down from the height of the throne at the crumpled figure sprawled motionlessly at his feet. There was nothing to fear from Zarkon, Lord of the Unknown, now. The gas that had rendered Zarkon unconscious was a potent nerve gas that acted by contact with the skin. You did not even have to breathe it in for it to act upon you.

Soon, in mere moments, Zarkon would struggle to consciousness again. But Lucifer feared nothing, for two guards stood to either side of him, their rifles leveled at the unconscious figure. Swift and clever as he was, Zarkon was helpless: The pointing rifles would hold him effectively at bay.

Odd, thought Lucifer with a cold smile, how the mighty Zarkon looked smaller than usual in so lowly a position! Erect, alert, in action, the man was as mighty as a colossus—a figure of awe and terror to evildoers. But now, in the ignominy of his final defeat, the slumped form looked shrunken and diminished.

The body of Zarkon had been tossed down unceremoniously at the foot of the throne in such a position that his face was turned away. The gloating eyes of Lucifer rested their scrutiny on the back of Zarkon's head. Those meticulously arranged locks of pewter-gray hair were disarranged now, he saw. And the flesh of Zarkon's nape caught his eye with its peculiar tint of saffron.

How many times, in the bitter loneliness of his cell, had he puzzled over the peculiar shade of Zarkon's skin, wondering what race or what mixture of races had produced the amazing superman who had become a living juggernaut, crushing supercriminal after supercriminal beneath his heel.

It annoyed him that he could not see the face of his helpless enemy. He would have delighted in gloating over the slack jaw, the lax lips, the closed eyes. And how it would have thrilled him to have the very first thing that Zarkon saw upon awakening from the drugged sleep be the triumphant visage of himself—Lucifer!

He almost bade his guards turn the man over so he could watch life and consciousness return to his face. But even as his lips parted to utter the curt command, the limp figure stirred, sighed, and began to waken.

Lucifer leaned forward, gripping the arms of his throne in an ecstasy of anticipation, watching hungrily as the huddled figure stirred to wakefulness.

By his side the rifles were leveled, covering the half-conscious man.

The figure of Zarkon tried to sit up. As it did so, its head sagged down dizzily, and the pewter-colored hairpiece fell off, revealing a hairless skull.

Lucifer smiled, taking pleasure in this small, undignified action. He knew, of course, that Zarkon's head was devoid of hair, although he had no idea why, and that the Man of Mysteries commonly wore a gray wig.

Now the bald, wobbling head lifted feebly, and

the man at the foot of the throne looked up weakly, stared up directly into the eyes of Lucifer—and gasped.

A similar, unbelieving cry broke from the lips of the mastermind of crime!

For the man who knelt before him, while he wore the garments of Zarkon, did not have the face of Zarkon.

It was the face of Ching!

At that precise moment, Scorchy Muldoon was staring with wide, unbelieving eyes into the face of a man he had never expected to see alive again.

It was Menlo Parker!

The wizened little scientist took his hand away from Scorchy's mouth and bent to saw through the nylon cord that bound his wrists behind him.

"Sure an' I'd be after swearin' 'tis a ghost ye are, Menlo, me pal," wheezed Scorchy in a faint voice, "were it not that me ould mither always taught her little Scorchy they was no sich things on this earth! Speak, Menlo—say somethin'—tell me ye're after bein' real!"

"Hesh up, you dumb Irishman!" spat the little scientist with his usual peevish bad temper. "Of course I'm real, you dopey Mick!"

Scorchy closed his eyes happily. " 'Tis yerself, Menlo, an' no skulkin' phantom, that's fer sure," he said, blissfully. "Is it alive ye are, then, an' that wicked fiend was after tellin' us as how he had struck ye down with th' Hand o' Death—"

"If you mean Lucifer, he thought he was telling the truth," snapped the frail little man. "He used the Hand of Death on me, all right, but something happened; dunno what. Damned thing didn't work for some reason. Happens I was watching his eyes after he had touched me, so just about the time I realized nothing was happening to me, I sensed from his expression the very moment he expected me to start yellin' . . . so, always happy to oblige a fiend, I started kickin' and squawkin' like a scaulded alley cat. Kept it up for thirty seconds, then slumped down and did my best to look deader'n a doornail. Fooled the big egotist, too, by golly! He had one of his thugs haul me off an' dump me in a storeroom. Soon as the lug's back was turned I knocked him cold with a karate chop to the nape of his ugly neck . . . musta clipped him harder than I really meant to, 'cause I broke his fool neck. So I just changed clothes with the corpse and snuck out of there in these dang-fool robes, with the hood pulled up so nobody could spot my kisser. I been sneakin' around in the shadows ever since, tryin' to keep out of sight. Saw 'em drag you birds in a while ago, so I stole the ring of keys, an' . . . there, by gosh, you're free. That nylon is danged tough stuff, lemme tell you!"

One by one, Scorchy Muldoon and Menlo Parker entered the other cells along the row and cut their friends loose. They gathered in the corridor outside, a sorry-looking bunch, in their shorts and socks. The unhappy expressions on their faces would have brought a smile to the lips of Elvira Higgins under less extraordinary circumstances, but the young lady was too grateful to be free and too tactful to comment on the appearance of the Omega men.

Nick Naldini flapped his long arms and shivered.

"Cold as the top drawer of a refrigerator out here, dressed like this," he complained dolefully. "Menlo, old sock, you're the miracle worker around here today—any chance of rustlin' us up some clothes?"

"Yeah," grinned Doc Jenkins happily, delighted at the unexpected resurrection of his friend. "For a guy that can come back from the grave, it ought to be a cinch to find us something to wear. I'd feel pretty silly, wadin' in to a fist fight with Lucifer's boys, dressed like a nudist who can't quite bring himself to go all the way!"

Menlo Parker sniffed spitefully. "The way you dumb bunnies just stood around twiddlin' your thumbs and let them crooks carry me off kickin' and screamin' and hangin' on to the bottom of that dad-ratted helicopter, it'd serve you right if I let you spend the rest of the day in your skivvies! But I just can't expose a delicate young female to all them skinny knees and bowlegs and flabby tummies, no sirree! You'll find a buncha these red bathrobes down in the room at the end. But for gosh sakes, don't disturb the guy I left snoozin' there! He'll be awful grouchy when he wakes up, on account of the goose egg I give him when I conked him on the noggin."

It didn't take the Omega men long to climb into the robes they found in the jailer's room. Within minutes they were slinking down the corridor, their hoods drawn up to cover their faces, with Elvira Higgins in the rear.

Doc Jenkins had kicked the jailer's chair apart so that they could all arm themselves with the kindling, which for the most part made pretty hefty cudgels. With considerable reluctance, Menlo had yielded his Bowie knife to Ace Harrigan, for the young aviator had picked up quite a knack at knife fighting during his vagabond years of knocking around the globe, and in his skillful hands the gleaming blade was a deadly weapon. Besides, Menlo now packed a .45, which he had shamelessly pilfered from the dead guard whose robe he also wore.

None of them had any idea where they were going, but with great good luck they did not happen to encounter any of Lucifer's thugs.

They suddenly turned a corner and found themselves staring upon a scene of dramatic confrontation.

There sat Lucifer on his high throne, two tall, towering Nubian guards at his side, their rifles leveled at the gray-clad figure who knelt at the foot of the throne.

None of them could possibly not have recognized that characteristic gray suede jacket and slacks or that bare skull with the pale golden hue. They knew their master when they saw him, or, at least, they thought they did.

"They got the chief!" roared Scorchy. "They're gonna shoot 'im down!"

Menlo whipped out his gun, leveled it at the bigger of the two guards, and snapped off a shot, winging him in the shoulder. The tall black went down, but in the same swift flurry of action, Lucifer whirled around behind the stone chair and vanished. The other guard lifted his rifle and fired at them point-blank. In the high-walled stone chamber the crash of gunfire resounded deafeningly.

What happened then was incredible—as incredible, that is, as it was unexpected.

The boom and gobble of echoes roared in the enclosed space.

The long, dangling, stony spears of the stalactites quivered like tuning forks and broke free. They fell like huge stone knives. One cracked the skull of the guard who had fired on the Omega men, and the other dropped to impale the kneeling figure in gray suede.

Horror sprang into the eyes of Menlo Parker. He stood as if he himself had been transfixed by one of the cold, sharp spears of stone. Dazedly he looked first at the man in gray, pinned to the ground like a moth under the quivering stalactite, then down at the smoking gun in his fist.

"O my God," he quavered, *"what have I done?"*

Chapter 21

Flaming Doom

Behind the great stone chair a trapdoor had been cut into the floor of Lucifer's throne room. It was covered by a stone slab that had a bronze ring affixed thereto so that it could be raised at will.

Lucifer had learned many years ago that it was wise to always have an escape route at hand. You never know when you are going to need one. So, even in his throne room, where he sat in state amid his secret fortress inside Mount Shasta, the mastermind of supercrime had an exit at hand.

When the red-robed men clustered in the doorway had fired, bringing down his trusted guard Mongo, the crime lord had seized the momentary distraction to get around behind the big stone chair. There, safe from flying bullets, he dragged open the trapdoor and vanished from view.

A black tunnel had been sunken down deep into the interior of the mountain. Steel rungs were clamped to one side of this vertical pit. Closing the trapdoor and bolting it securely above him, Lucifer descended into the darkness, rung by rung.

At the bottom, the tunnel opened out into a horizontal stone corridor, which the genius of crime followed to its end. There a fully equipped chemical laboratory was housed in a square stone chamber. Porcelain benches drawn up along the walls held a sparkling array of crystal tubing, flasks, crucibles and Bunsen burners. It was in this room that Ching prepared the subtle poison that was the secret of the Hand of Death.

Here, too, a televisor screen was set into one wall. Lucifer crossed over to it and peered within its glowing circle. The Omega men, he observed grimly, had seized the upper hand and were rapidly gaining control of the entire system of tunnels and rooms that comprised the secret headquarters of Lucifer.

Manipulating the control verniers, the big man looked into room after room. He saw Ching and Mongo in shackles, the Eurasian wounded in the rockfall being bandaged by the Omega men. Switching to views of other parts of his stronghold, the crime lord saw that Menlo Parker had put to good use his hours of freedom. The wrinkled little scientist had led his comrades to the central controls, and even as Lucifer watched through the glowing televisor screen, steel grilles were clanging down to block passageways and seal off rooms, cutting Lucifer's horde of red-robed thugs into small, helpless, captive groups. Parker had only to release the sleep gas into these rooms and the hidden citadel was conquered.

But all was not yet lost! Lucifer still lived and was hidden. And there were still certain weapons that were his last aces in the hole. The dynamite charges buried beneath key pillars and walls, for example. All he had to do was to close the red switch at his left hand, and the peak of Mount Shasta would be rocked by a sequence of explosions so destructive, so devastating, that none of them would escape with their lives.

Lucifer reached out to grasp the red lever. As he did so, a steely voice spoke from behind him.

"It will do you no good; the wires have been severed."

Lucifer turned. Zarkon stood there, still wearing the red robe he had taken from Ching, when he had quickly changed clothes with the unconscious Eurasian back in the power room.

"I have made the dangerous mistake of underestimating you, Prince Zarkon!" said Lucifer, gravely. "I beg your pardon for having done so. This round is yours, I admit."

Zarkon nodded, saying nothing. In one hand he held a revolver.

"I understand now that you switched clothing with my servant, Ching," said Lucifer. "Doubtless, this was accomplished in the few short moments the televisor lenses were blinded by the gush of anesthetic vapor into the power room. But, tell me: How did you escape from the room? I had already closed off all exits from the chamber by lowering the steel grilles."

"I did not escape at all," said Zarkon. "I merely retreated from the path of the vapor and concealed myself behind one of the big turbines in the far corner until the gas dissipated. Then I simply waited until your thugs entered the chamber, and mingled unobtrusively with them until such time as I could leave the chamber without anyone noticing my movements."

"And how came you here, might I ask, to my most secret and hidden adytum?" Lucifer inquired in a stony voice.

Zarkon rarely smiled, but in this instance his

magnetic black eyes twinkled with something approaching humor.

"By accident," he confessed. "I really wasn't trying to find your hiding place of last resort at all, I was simply trying to keep out of sight. I passed the throne room, looked in, and happened to spot the trapdoor. Just then your two tame giants—"

"Mongo and Simba? My Nubian blacks?"

Zarkon nodded. "It must have been them. They came into the throne room. I ducked down behind the dais and decided to go down through the trapdoor before they got a glimpse of me. Quite frankly, I had no idea of what this place was, other than that it was your laboratory for chemical experiments. I had no idea you would come ducking down here yourself, before very long."

"I see," Lucifer nodded. "Again, sir, my congratulations! You are far more resourceful and ingenious than I would have believed. I fail to understand, however, how your agent, Dr. Parker, survived the Hand of Death unharmed. . . ."

"I discovered the nature of the poison when I performed an autopsy on the bodies of your murdered henchmen," Zarkon replied quietly. "As you must know, the pharmacopoeia contains a common drug that is a specific against the poison. I took a bottle from the police laboratory and gave my men a dose in their coffee before we left the headquarters. The dose was sufficient to immunize them for several hours, at least. Since I had already come to suspect that the newspaper publisher, Ryan, was a member of your organization, I said nothing about the immunization to my men at the time, of course."

"So Parker was quick-thinking enough to fake the convulsions, even though he had no advance knowledge of the fact that the Hand of Death could not harm him," mused Lucifer. "A clever man! You are the master of a superb organization, Prince Zarkon . . . if only I could persuade you to join forces with me! Together, we could conquer the world; together, we could share its rule."

Zarkon shook his head without hesitation.

"That can never be," he said. "It was to destroy such dreams of empire, by such men as you, that I was sent here in the first place. We must forever be adversaries, Lucifer, until one of us destroys the other. . . ."

Lucifer grinned, snatching up a heavy glass beaker filled with virulent green fluid. His action was so swiftly performed, so perfectly timed, that it took Zarkon unawares.

"An event that may take place much sooner than you think, Prince!" he sneered. Zarkon elevated the revolver.

"I can shoot you where you stand," said the Ultimate Man quietly.

"If you do, my friend, you will destroy yourself, as well as me," smiled the bald, bullet-headed man in the voluminous silken robes whose color was the hue of human blood. "For this beaker contains a powerful acid of my own invention! Were I to hurl it at you—which I would do, if even with my dying breath—you would be destroyed instantly. While I might well survive your bullet. You have, of course, no way of telling whether or not I am wearing a bulletproof jacket underneath these robes of mine."

"That is true," admitted Zarkon, lowering the revolver slowly.

"Very well, then. Drop your gun and kick it over to me. All I wish is to escape from this place. I am willing to let you live, as well, for I envision that on another day we shall both cross swords once again. Drop your weapon, I say, and you may leave here unharmed—attempt to put a bullet through me, and I will destroy you with this chemical. Choose: but quickly! My patience is nearly at its end."

Zarkon stared thoughtfully at his archenemy. He stared also at the Bunsen burner just behind Lucifer on the porcelain table from which the mastermind of crime had snatched up the flask of acid.

Without a word or the slightest flicker of expression, Zarkon bent down and deposited the revolver on the stone floor.

"Ah!" exclaimed Lucifer, with satisfaction. "Now you are acting wisely, my friend! Come, kick the pistol over to me. . . ."

Zarkon did so. Lucifer half turned to set the beaker down on the table, and in the next moment he would have stooped to pick up the revolver that Zarkon had surrendered. But the act was never completed.

As he half turned, the voluminous sleeves of his robes brushed the Bunsen burner, where a small gas flame burned unnoticed. The thin silken fabric of the scarlet robes caught fire instantaneously.

Lucifer's robe became a mass of flames!

The mastermind of crime screamed once, his grim, powerful face distorted with rage and pain and horror. He thrust his hands out blindly, as if to stave off the doom whose seething flames enveloped him.

But he still held the acid beaker!

It crashed to the floor at his feet, and burst into a thousand glittering shards against the smooth stone.

The flaming hem of Lucifer's robes touched the spreading pool of acid, which hissed as it ate into the smooth rock of the floor.

The explosion rocked the room and brought the roof crashing down.

Only a split second before the explosion, Zarkon sprang into action. Moving so swiftly that to the human eye his flying form would have been but a blur, the Lord of the Unknown whipped out of the room and into the corridor beyond.

There he whirled, diving behind a stout stone column about as thick as the trunk of a mighty oak.

The explosion resounded deafeningly. A sheet of flame blazed through the open door. It licked out for many feet, and had Zarkon still been traveling in that direction, his own scarlet robes would have been ignited and consumed. As it was, although stunned by the explosion and momentarily deafened, he was otherwise unharmed.

Retreating back down the corridor, the Ultimate Man took one last look into the laboratory. It had been transformed into a raging inferno. Nothing could possibly have lived for more than an instant in that roaring holocaust. It was like looking into the open mouth of a blast furnace.

If Lucifer was still within, his body must have been burned to ash by now.

The words of ominous warning that Lucifer had earlier uttered to Menlo Parker were now proved prophetic. His devilish cavern world truly contained hellfire. And in that seething inferno, Lucifer himself had been consumed!

Although a grim and ghastly fate, it was a fitting end for the ruthless mastermind of criminality, who had dared assume the name of the archfiend as his pseudonym.

Lucifer, the Prince of Hell, whose dominion is the Inferno itself!

In that searing hellfire, the archenemy of civilization had suffered his final defeat, ending in self-destruction. It was a termination to his career in crime that Zarkon found curiously apt. It could almost have been called "poetic justice."

But Zarkon was not exhilarated by his victory. The tall man stood somberly, a brooding expression on his classically handsome features. His eyes were enshadowed by an emotion that was almost regret.

Was it regret for the maniac whose madness had first perverted and then destroyed a brilliant intellect, a great career, a life of enormous potential value to mankind?

Or was it the gentlemanly instinct of the sportsman, who acknowledges the demise of a great adversary, the passing of a foeman worthy of his steel?

No one can say. At that moment his face was unreadable, an enigma, sphinxlike in its inscrutability.

Chapter 22

The Case is Closed

Yes, Zarkon would not have been Zarkon had he not regretted the passing of his archenemy, Lucifer. That so brilliant a brain had destroyed itself seemed to him lamentable—almost as lamentable as the fact that a genius of science had transformed himself into a genius of crime. Had Lucifer been taken alive, it was not beyond possibility that his mighty intellect might have been converted from the paths of criminality to the service of humanity. His death had made an end to a career of great though evil deeds. Zarkon was relieved that the tyranny that Lucifer schemed had failed to enslave the civilization of the world, but he was saddened at the destruction of such a giant intellect.

And yet it was to destroy such men as this that Zarkon had been sent here, years ago.

The secret of Zarkon's mysterious origin was known to but a few. It must forever remain a secret.

Zarkon turned his back on the burning laboratory that had become the funeral pyre of Lucifer and his mad schemes of world domination, retraced the narrow tunnel to its beginning, and climbed the steel rungs to the top. Unbolting the trapdoor, he opened it, climbed out, and surveyed the wreckage.

One of Lucifer's two black bodyguards had been shot, but not fatally, from the noise the ebony giant was making as Ace Harrigan attempted to bandage his wounds.

Ching, too, had somehow managed to survive the crippling descent of the pointed stone stalactite. The brittle point of the dangling spear had broken his shoulder and pierced the muscles, but had narrowly missed severing the great artery that leads to the heart. Had he been kneeling a handbreadth to the left at the moment the explosion of gunfire brought the jagged stones crashing down, the suave little Eurasian would not have survived to pay the penalty for his complicity in Lucifer's dreams of empire.

Menlo Parker had succeeded in stanching the flow of blood, and had extracted the point of the stalactite. Now he knelt at the side of the unconscious little man who had been unwittingly cast into the role of Zarkon and whose imposture had gone unexposed until the last moment. The oriental chemist lay still, breathing stertorously, his amber complexion waxen from shock or loss of blood.

Menlo glanced up, jumped, and swore.

"Chief! Where the Sam Hill'd *you* come from? Dang near scared the life out of me, popping up out of nowhere like that!"

Zarkon nodded in the direction of the trapdoor.

Menlo nodded thoughtfully. "Thought that's where you might be, somehow. Lucifer ducked out that way, didn't he? Musta bolted the blame thing from underneath; we couldn't budge it. Doc's gone to fetch a crowbar right now, so's we could pry the blamed thing open. Lucifer didn't get away, did he?"

Zarkon shook his head somberly. Menlo seemed satisfied with that, and asked no further questions. He finished bandaging the wounded Eurasian and climbed to his feet wearily.

"What a night this has been! Feel so tired I could sleep for a week."

"How is Ching?" asked Zarkon. Menlo shrugged carelessly.

"He'll live to go to prison, I guess," he said. "You sure fooled us all with that change of clothes bit. How'd you work it so fast?"

"My garments are not held together with zippers or buttons," Zarkon explained, "but with adhesive strips. I have practiced the trick before, to perfect my timing. I can effect a complete transition in a remarkably short time. Such things sometimes can come in handy."

Menlo opened his mouth to make some reply, but just then the other Omega men came in, Doc Jenkins lugging the no-longer-needed crowbar. They greeted their leader jubilantly, crowding around to welcome him happily.

"Boyoboyoboy! Chief, you oughta see it. Never seen anythin' like it, begorra!" Scorchy burbled joyously. "We got inta the central control room and let down all them steel grilles. Seems like just about ever' dad-gone doorway in th' place is tricked out with 'em. We got ever' single last one o' Lucifer's gang locked up—and right here in they own secret hidey hole, too!"

The sun was well up into the sky before they emerged at length from the caverns into the open air and the light of day. It was midmorning before

Chief Patterson's state troopers had gotten the last
of Lucifer's gang members down the steep stairstep-
like slope of the mountainside and into the paddy
wagons that were drawn up at the foot of Mount
Shasta· to receive them. There was a miniature
fleet of the security vehicles, for Lucifer's thugs
numbered two score. ·

Eventually the last gang member had been
rounded up, handcuffed, escorted into the last
paddy wagon, and been driven away, siren clamor-
ing victoriously. Of course, there was still much to
be done. It would probably take the state police the
better part of a week to comb through the
caverns to their last nook and cranny, examine
and itemize the last morsel of evidence, and cart it
away. The cleaning up, they knew, usually takes
more time in such cases than does the process of
busting the case wide open.

"By golly, that dad-ratted mountain!" swore the
fat, red-faced officer, mopping his streaming brow
with his fiery-hued bandanna and fanning himself
vigorously with the bit of damp cloth. "If I gotta
go up an' down that dang heap o' rocks one more
time, I swear to gosh I'm gonna turn in my
badge! Always thought them mountain climber
fellows was nuts; now I *know* blamed well they
are. Enough to give a fellow the conniption-fits,
all this climbin' up and down!"

"Did you find the helicopter?" inquired Zarkon.

"That we did! Dad-blastid thing was hid in a
sort of hangar with big doors, way up above the
rest o' these goldurned tunnels," snorted the state
cop. "Coupla wiseguys we caught tryin' to make a
sneaky takeoff, but we nailed 'em. Guess we got
about all th' crooks rounded up by now. Gotta
hand it to you and yer boys, Prince; you sure done a

swell job. Gol-ding it, just wait'll the newspapers
get ahold of this one! It'll sure be a real feather in
yer cap, by golly!"

Zarkon looked acutely uncomfortable. He cleared
his throat apologetically.

"Chief Patterson," he said solemnly, "I would
be greatly obliged to you if our role in this affair
was played down. I would really be much happier
if you and your officers were to take the lion's
share of the credit for breaking this gang."

The fat man looked astonished. Zarkon assured
him that he and his lieutenants would be more than
willing to give full details on the operation, but
preferred to keep their part in the adventure as
secret as possible.

"Publicity is the last thing we desire," he informed the state cop. "The less that is publicly
known about us, the better we can fight crime now
and in the future. I am more than willing that
you should take all the credit in this instance."

For once the red-faced officer was too flabber-
gasted to loose his usual torrent of amusingly in-
offensive epithets.

Just a moment later, Chief Patterson's red face
grew solemn, and he removed his sweat-stained old
Stetson and held it over his heart. The stretcher
bearers were bringing down the corpse of Robert
Russell Ryan.

"That's a ding-blastid shame," the state cop muttered. "A good man like him; shore makes a feller
wish that dod-rotted crook, Lucifer, weren't dead,
too. Shore would like to send the feller up fer life,
killin' Mr. Ryan that way. He were a mighty good
man!"

Zarkon said nothing. He had told Chief Patter-

son only that the millionaire publisher had died in
the scuffle, but he had kept silent on the matter of
Ryan's complicity in Lucifer's plot, and his part
in the conspiracy. After all, the man was dead. He
could not be punished for his role in the mystery
murders—why, then, should his name and reputation be blasted?

Zarkon intended to say nothing to the authorities
about the Judas role of Robert Russell Ryan. Let
him go to his grave remembered for the good and
constructive things he had done with his life. Let
his secret die with him.

They left the foot of Mount Shasta and drove
back to the Ryan estate in Seagrove. Later on that
day, or perhaps on the day following, they would
have to make their statements for the police records. Then they would be free to return to Knickerbocker City. Chief Patterson had told Prince
Zarkon that simultaneous raids on the lodges of the
Brotherhood had netted the missing members of
Lucifer's Circle of Disciples, who were indeed
wanted men with long criminal records. The lodges
had been closed after the raid and would not re-
open. The whole gang was under lock and key,
including the Eurasian chemist, Ching, and Mongo,
the giant black. After a simple inquest, the case
would be closed.

"I shore will see to it that that dad-ratted
Chinaman gits locked up fer life," swore Chief
Patterson feelingly, as they drove away. "Just in
case he gits any ideas of settin' himse'f up in
business as 'Lucifer, Jr.' You boys finished thar?"

"Yep, that's it, Chief," said one of his officers.
The man was staring after Zarkon's car as it drove
away.

"What's the story on that Prince guy?" inquired

the officer. "You really going to keep his name out of all this, Chief?"

Orville Patterson fixed the younger man with a hard glare.

"Yew take yer hat off, sonny, when yew talk about Prince Zarkon!" he said heavily. "He's the bes' natural-born cop I ever set eyes on! Ding-bust it all, if I had five like him on th' force, the sovereign state o' Californy'd be mos' law-abidin' state this side o' Shangri-la. You hear me talkin'?"

"Yessir, Chief!"

"Then *git*."

The young officer saluted smartly, and "got." And never thereafter did Chief Orville Patterson of the state police cease reminiscing about his friendship with the mysterious Novenian nobleman, and how they had once worked hand-in-glove together on the *dangdest* crime in state history.

Chapter 23

The Man from Tomorrow

It was noon before Zarkon and the Omega men and Elvira Higgins got back to the estate of the late Robert Russell Ryan in the fashionable Seagrove suburb of Palma Laguna. They were hungry, dirty, disheveled, and bone weary after the long night of adventure, imprisonment, and battle.

Anxious as to the outcome of their mysterious venture, the managing editor of Ryan's newspaper, the Los Angeles *Illustrated Press,* had driven over from that city and awaited them on the front steps of the mansion.

They had not seen Gordon Halleck, he of the nervous and prodigious eyebrows, since their first arrival here in the *Shooting Star.* The editor was sobered by the news of the untimely demise of his employer. In a solemn voice he asked for details, and listened in a subdued manner while Zarkon quietly told him a spurious account of his employer's heroism in their battle against the criminal Brotherhood and a few sketchy and unobtrusively inaccurate details surrounding the moment of his death.

After shaking hands all around and tendering his awkward thanks, the editor drove back to Los

211

Angeles to write the story. Zarkon had managed
to persuade him to avoid any mention of the Omega
organization in his newspaper account of the case,
suggesting that all of the credit be given to the dead
reporter, for digging up the facts in the first place,
and to Chief Orville Patterson of the state police
for raiding the local branches of the gang and
grabbing the rest of the crooks right in their very
stronghold.

Then he and his lieutenants and their guest,
Miss Elvira Higgins, sat down to an enormous hot
meal, which they devoured with gusto, while the
servants of the late Robert Russell Ryan prepared
hot baths in which to soak their weary limbs after
the completion of their repast.

After bathing, a good long nap, and a change
into clean clothes, they had to write out their statements for Chief Patterson, who sent an officer
around in a squad car to pick up the documents
needed as court evidence. The chief informed them
by telephone that afternoon that they would not
be required to attend the inquest nor to give their
testimony in open court at the trial of the gangsters.
This was certainly good news, because Zarkon and
the Omega men wished to keep their names out of
the case as completely as could possibly be done.

After an early dinner, they began to pack up for
their return flight to Knickerbocker City.

While his lieutenants gathered their gear together and began to repack the big equipment
cases they had brought with them, Zarkon went
off by himself for a stroll in the garden. There
were times when the Lord of the Unknown preferred to be alone with his thoughts. And this was
one of them.

Sunset flamed in the west, painting the clouds with gold and crimson, and lighting a clear and luminous evening sky with gorgeous rays. From the garden you could just make out the snowy peak of Mount Shasta, which was barely visible in the distance.

Zarkon strolled the garden paths, his hands clasped behind him, his inscrutable face and brooding eyes reflecting nothing of the tenor of his thoughts.

The Ultimate Man always felt a certain depression of his spirits when he had been forced to destroy an enemy. Foolish as it perhaps may seem, he bitterly regretted the necessity for taking a single human life—even the life of a criminal mastermind such as Dr. Zandor Sinestro, or Lucifer, the aptly named genius of crime whom civilization was much better off for being rid of.

True, Zarkon was not personally responsible for the fiery death of Lucifer—that is, he had not killed the crime lord with his own hands. Nevertheless, he felt himself morally culpable and did not enjoy the feeling.

However, it was to bring down such Napoleons of the Underworld as Lucifer, and to wreck their plots and schemes against the security of the world, that he had been sent here years ago, and he knew that his moody depression and vague sensations of guilt were silly.

The secret origin of Zarkon, Lord of the Unknown, was known to very few. You could, in fact, count upon the fingers of both hands the number of living men who shared the secret of who and what he really was, where he had come from, and for what mysterious purpose.

That tremendous secret must ever be closely

guarded. It must forever be the jealously-hidden possession of a few.

From no nation on our Earth today did Zarkon come.

By no year in the calendar of our history could his birth be reckoned.

He was a man from a far-off time, come from the distant future of another age to help us in combating the criminal masterminds who threaten and imperil the peace of the world and the security of all nations.

Zarkon had been born a million years from now, in a strange and mysterious future world.

He represented the ultimate result of a program of genetic engineering conducted by the rulers of his weird world of tomorrow to protect against the extinction of the human race.

Superhuman, rather than human, he was the end result of an experiment in selective breeding conducted over thousands of generations to produce a perfect superman.

In that remote era, life was almost extinct on the Earth. Unbridled pollution of air and water, uncontrolled wastage of natural resources, endless millennia of warfare and ecological depletion had left the Earth exhausted, sterile, very nearly uninhabitable.

Only in the artificial domed city of Polarion in the Arctic regions did a haven of enlightened scientific civilization still exist. Save for that domed paradise, the rest of the world was barren wilderness where roved ever-dwindling hordes of savage barbarians.

The Great Brains of Polarion had searched backward in their history for the roots of the disaster that had all but destroyed the world. These supercomputers, in whose memory banks the totality of human knowledge was preserved, had discovered the cause of the collapse of human civilization. It lay in the closing decades of the Twentieth Century. In that long-forgotten age there had arisen to power in the interval between two global conflicts, criminal masterminds who had exploited the superstitious fears of the people through the use of advanced scientific secrets.

When urban civilization disintegrated after the nuclear holocaust of the third such worldwide conflict, it was these sinister supermen of organized crime who had seized the reins of power and who divided the world among them in the ensuing Dark Ages of plague and famine and lawlessness that followed in the wake of the collapse of legitimate governments.

The Great Brains resolved upon a daring scheme to change the present, and save the future, by *undoing the past*. For a quarter of a million years they had selectively bred a race of supermen, called "Arkons," to rule the dwindling remnants of mankind. But this program had reached its fruition too late, as the planet was nearly dead. Therefore, the last of these experimental supermen, Arkon Z-1000, was projected backward in time to the Twentieth Century. It was his mighty mission to prevent the rise to power of the scientific supercriminals, so that the feudal dark ages would not attend the destruction of civilization.

It had been a conspiracy of such men that had triggered the third and final holocaust, the Great Brains knew. A gigantic conspiracy of these secret crime lords had wrecked the world's governments. To change the future, Zarkon—Arkon Z-1000—

must change the past. To prevent the destruction of the world, he must prevent the nuclear war.

Calling himself "Zarkon," the Man from Tomorrow had materialized first in the small Balkan country of Novenia, a tiny but strategic state that controlled the world's only known source of the rare heavy metal rhombium, vital to the generation of atomic power and the construction of nuclear weapons. The processes by which rhombium was refined were slow, expensive, and crude; using his knowledge of future science, Zarkon swiftly introduced a process for the refinement of the rare metal that was cheap, easy, and fast.

Virtually overnight, Novenia became wealthy and powerful and influential on a global scale because of her control of the rhombium mines and refinement process. Named a national hero by the grateful Novenian people, the scientist Zarkon was elevated to power by them. The extinct monarchy, long supplanted by a shaky succession of military regimes, was revived, with Zarkon crowned by unanimous popular consent.

Zarkon remained on the throne of Novenia for only a few years, long enough to reform the economy, subdue the military party, equalize the taxation, and engineer a number of international treaties that insured the future of Novenia as an independent sovereign state, neither under the domination of the East nor a client of the West. Then the Man of Mysteries had abdicated the throne, establishing a perfect model democracy to succeed his reign and authoring a constitution that was enlightened and permanent.

His work in Novenia done, Prince Zarkon had come to the United States to set up his Omega organization and begin the great work that would occupy him for the rest of his life.

These memories passed through the mind of the Lord of the Unknown as he paced the dark gardens under the blazing stars.

The loneliness that he knew, this exile of time, was not to be measured by comparison to that of any man. Of all men who have ever lived on this Earth, he alone was a stranger from the future—a future to which he could never return, for by his own actions he was destroying that future by changing its past. With every adventure such as this case of the Mount Shasta murders, he was destroying the future world he had known and building a new future that he would never see. Happily, it would be a world whose resources had not been exhausted by interminable feudal wars, whose population had not been degraded and brutalized by thralldom to generations of tyrants and despots. He dreamed sometimes of the idyllic, crime-free garden world his labors were constructing—a world where crime was unknown, dictatorship a forgotten trait, war an ancient horror long since outlawed.

A voice hailed him from the big house. Breaking off his thoughts, the Lord of the Unknown retraced his steps and entered the mansion.

"Everything's packed up, chief; we're ready to go. The lady wants to say goodbye," said Doc Jenkins. Zarkon nodded without speaking. Miss Elvira Higgins was ready to return home to Palma Laguna and was making her farewells to the Omega men.

Menlo Parker, that old woman-hater, sniffed frostily and inclined his head in the barest semblance of a nod as the young woman said goodbye. Scorchy Muldoon and Nick Naldini, however, were more voluble in their farewells. Both men had tried without success to get a date with the attractive redhead; she had demurely declined the invitation of either man. As soon as Zarkon entered the room, anyone could have seen why, from the long, lingering, starry-eyed look she gave him as they shook hands.

Doc Jenkins and Ace Harrigan exchanged secret grins. It was always like this—Nick and Scorchy vied for the attentions of whatever pretty girl shared an adventure with them, but the girl, once she set eyes on the tall and handsome man in gun-metal gray, fell for Zarkon and ignored the peppery little Irishman and the lanky stage magician.

It was a real waste, thought Doc Jenkins, chuckling to himself. The Ultimate Man possessed some mysterious magnetic charm where women were concerned, but never took advantage of his power. Obviously, he felt a crime-fighting career was nothing for a woman to get mixed up in. Probably, he was right.

Miss Higgins bade Prince Zarkon a reluctant goodbye, and left with many a backward look. Zarkon, who had been looking uncomfortable and embarrassed in the attractive redhead's presence, now seemed relieved. He virtually breathed a sigh of relief once the pretty girl had left the house!

"Guess we're all ready, chief," grinned Ace Harrigan.

"Then let's get going! I have no doubt there will be new cases waiting for us when we get back to Knickerbocker City," said the Man of Mysteries.

Scorchy and Nick Naldini were quarreling loudly as they all went trooping out of the mansion and down to the airfield where their plane was waiting, fueled and ready.

"You phony vaudeville ham, you scared her off with all that leering and hand kissing!" complained Scorchy. "If you hadn't been around all the time, I bet I coulda got a date."

"You pea-brained pugilist, it was you who was in the way," snarled the magician. "I tell you, she was giving me the glad eye, but you queered the deal."

"Oh, yeah? You tank-town Houdini, I'll curl yer mustache for ya!"

"You and what other twelve pugs, you Gaelic goon?"

"Boy, we better find some more action quick, before those two tear into each other," breathed Doc Jenkins to his chief.

The Nemesis of Evil smiled but said nothing.